Mysteries Squared

Russ Hall

Mysteries Squared
Red Adept Publishing, LLC
104 Bugenfield Court
Garner, NC 27529
https://RedAdeptPublishing.com/
Copyright © 2023 by Russ Hall. All rights reserved.
Cover Art by Streetlight Graphics[1]

This is a work of fiction. Names, characters, places, and incidents either are the product of the author's imagination or are used fictitiously, and any resemblance to locales, events, business establishments, or actual persons—living or dead—is entirely coincidental.

---

1.   http://StreetlightGraphics.com

Chapter 1: The Same Old, Same Old

Nothing ever happened around there.

Except for Jake Marston being found chopped up in large pieces that ended up scattered around half of Travis County. Esbeth wouldn't have been involved at all if she hadn't found an arm in the Coreopsis. She didn't know it was Jake's when she found it, just knew it probably belonged to someone.

"Esbeth Walters!" Mrs. McCorkle leaned out her window to yell at her from the place next door. "You get inside and put on a bonnet before you catch your death of the rays." Esbeth waved an irritated hand at her, the biddy. Folks thought that if you were in your seventies and you lived alone, you were bound to be dotty. McCorkle was barely sixty, thought she knew everything, and was far too willing to share her pearly wisdom.

Esbeth liked spring wildflowers, a reason for living in central Texas a lot of folks didn't know about, she figured, or a whole lot more of them would be crowding around in the area than already were. She'd been tromping around in the late stages of the bluebonnets, enjoying the Indian paintbrush, brown-eyed Susans, and pink primrose, when she had her anatomical encounter with Jake's arm. It lay there among the feathery green stems, a hairy and muscular appendage that hadn't bled much. Where it had been severed beneath the armpit, it had been smashed by something heavy, a brutal and powerful blow that had closed the wound as it created it.

She had half a notion not to go inside. Doing so might give old Big Nose too much satisfaction. Besides, she had to put in a call to Sheriff Danvers.

Deputy Bob Clanton arrived at her place twenty minutes later. He went with her to where she'd found the arm and told her on the way about other folks finding pieces of Jake. Esbeth could see old McCorkle sticking her beak between venetian blinds she held apart with two fingers. She'd have given worlds for her to know what they were looking at. That would have scalded her preserves.

"They already made an ID on some of the other parts," Bob said, making conversation. The arm lay there like an orphan between them. In return, Esbeth pointed out an early stand of Mexican hat blooms swaying in a clump on their tall stems high up on a hill near them. Folks other than McCorkle thought an old maid like Esbeth was prone to be a bit ditsy, too, and she'd found through the years that it was to her advantage to let them think so.

"Now I know you had a little taste of success there when you meddled in that Fergusson case where you ought'n to have." Bob Clanton stood there, one hand on his hip, the other forearm resting on the butt of his gun, acting as if his badge weighed a ton. "But I want to caution you now to keep clear of this. You lay folk think there's no risk to a murder case. Trust me. I know different. Leave this one to us men."

Oh, she was mad enough to snap a cracker. But she took a deep breath before she dared speak. "Do you ever wonder," she finally managed, "why it is you never hear a woman say she'd like to get in touch with her masculine side?"

He just gave her that twisted-mouth look. The one folks saved for the mentally infirm.

Meddled in the Fergusson case, my eye! They had been so far off the track in that one that it had taken her quite a bit of explaining to convince them that Lex Fergusson would ever dream of putting small doses of rat poison in his wife's food for nearly a year. Then a crew of hot shots from the state CID unit had come in, proved her right. You'd have thought she was the luckiest-guessing old coot alive. But she'd been watching Lex longer than they had, had seen him getting oily and nicer during the past year, the way someone would when the other shoe was about to drop and in his favor.

The medical examiner's crew pulled up, lights flashing. The year was 1984, and George Orwell was nowhere in sight, but the police were, if anything, enthusiastic.

"I understand," Deputy Bob said to her. They watched a swarm of cops go crashing through the flowers she'd formerly been enjoying. They had brought an entire EMS vehicle to collect the one arm. "You want to prove you can still contribute, do some good. Well, that's okay, as long as you don't get in the way. But some of the time you might try to act less batty. Not all of us fall for it."

She had nothing to say to that. Sure, she had her deflector shields up. Most people didn't see through that as well as Deputy Bob. You see, she didn't always enjoy the company of other people the way old farts were supposed to, especially crowds.

"Just give this one a rest," Bob said.

Well, she did, for about an hour. Then she made a call and hustled downtown. The place you wanted to go if you ever wanted to turn over the rock of any town was the newspaper office. Soon she was waving away clouds of Chesterfield smoke as Scottie tilted back his coffee cup with one hand while waving over the waitress with his cigarette hand. She didn't even know where he got the darn things anymore, probably had them ordered in special. The waitress filled their cups again. Scottie was the staff photographer for Austin's version of the *Daily Planet* and fancied himself something of a wit as well. They sat in the diner that was attached like a barnacle to the newspaper building. From the smell, Esbeth gathered the cook was a frequent fryer.

"Some people smoke 'em as short as they can," he said, nodding toward the dwindling non-filter butt in the yellowed ends of his fingers. "I smoke 'em as long as I can." He grinned. She smiled, too, though that was about four or five hundred times for her hearing that one from him. His jaded lines aside, he was a good newshound. He was tracking the room around them without knowing it, could have written a detailed description later that would have surprised him more than her.

"So, what's the skinny on the Marstons?" Esbeth asked when she thought the meal she'd bought him had had a chance to settle and he was done being a court jester.

"What do you know about the Hatfields and McCoys?"

"Depends. Which was Jake?" She had the feeling that this was going to be one of those that started off seeming simple then wasn't.

"Why do you want to know?"

Scottie had been one of her students when she taught high school math back about a light year ago. He'd also taken her picture during the Fergusson splash just last year, but like everyone else, he had her figured for past it.

"Call me curious." She could tell from the glitter in his eyes he had a story he was dying to share anyway.

"The Marstons and the Svensons have been going at it tooth and tong since Texas was a Republic." He drew another cigarette from the pack in his shirt pocket, lit it from the stub of the one going. "Some think that had to do with Rufus disappearing the way he did, leaving Sadie with the three kids to raise. There were Jake, Jeremy, and Sue Belle."

"How many Svensons are there?"

"Now only one. Ged Svenson. He has a butcher shop on South Lamar."

"Doesn't sound like much of a feud."

"That part of it sure isn't," Scottie puffed and agreed. He tilted his head back in silent laughter then lowered his glittering eyes back to her. "Ged hasn't made so much as a bark at the Marstons. Losing most of the Svensons kind of dried up the feud. Being naturally a scrappy lot, then the Marston family started in on each other. The fighting got so bad none of them had spoken to each other in years—that is, until last Thanksgiving."

Esbeth waited, in spite of sucking up enough secondhand smoke to shorten her antique life by a year.

"Sue Belle came into the newspaper office with an obituary written up on her brother Jake."

"But Jake wasn't dead... then."

"Right. But we didn't know that at the time. No one had ever brought in a fake obituary on a family member before. We published it. Jake stormed into the newspaper office the next day, made quite a stink. Turns out Sue Belle was just trying to reconcile the family, get them on speaking terms again. Figured if they all showed up for the funeral, it would be the first time they'd had Thanksgiving together in all that time. Maybe it would bring them closer."

"Did it?" Esbeth felt set up, guessing from the twinkling eye that got her.

"Turned into a real donnybrook, Jeremy smashing a coffee table over Jake, Jake going to his truck for a gun. In the struggle that followed, Jeremy got shot in the leg, still limps."

Chapter 2: Not a Big Crowd

Esbeth carried the scene of the family's little domestic discord with her to the funeral parlor that evening. There was to be a viewing, closed coffin as it turned out. Big surprise. Also worthy of note, Jeremy was a mortician, but the casket was at a competing funeral home. Esbeth was not much on funerals, but she wanted to catch a family member or two. Besides, she had a nifty little black outfit she wanted to wear, though on her build these days it looked more Dolly Parton than Donna Karan.

Sue Belle was the only Marston visible. She was blond, delicate in spite of filling out the black dress she wore in a more rounded way than Esbeth's. A fine flower of the South, that Sue Belle, with soft, very pale skin that seemed a stark white in contrast to the mascara streaks running down her cheeks.

There were just the two of them in there, kind of a lonely wake so far. "Thanks ever so much for coming," she said when she had choked back the tears and realized Esbeth was hovering at the back of the room. Sue Belle moved up closer. Her right arm was in a white sling.

"Momma's been by earlier," she explained, embarrassed by the poor family showing. "She's took it real hard."

Esbeth reeled back a half step but struggled not to show it. Sue Belle was one of the millions who thought vodka had no smell.

"Do you want to take a little walk?" Esbeth asked. "Give it a break for a while."

"Sure." Sue Belle leaned her free arm on Esbeth's and almost all her weight with it as if she had been waiting for someone to lean on. They went outside. The air seemed cooler and fresher after Esbeth was around the flowers and funeral parlor smell, though it was still pretty warm out.

"Who could have done a thing like that to Jake?" Esbeth asked.

"I don't know," she said before Niagara kicked in again. When she finally ran dry and had used up two of her hankies and Esbeth's, she asked, "Are you with the law or somethin'?"

Imagine, thinking that of someone old as Esbeth. "No. Just trying to help out."

A lot of folks would get their backs up about that. Sue Belle just said, "That's good. Someone oughta."

"Do you think it might go back to that feud your family once had with the Svensons?"

Sue Belle leaped at that. "It well might."

Esbeth had made a swing to the south end of town after her visit with Scottie, had stopped in at the Svenson butcher shop. Ged was something to see, a mountain of a fellow. He seemed to have eaten something sour for lunch, or else was on a permanent mad. He had to be six-four or -five, with the bulk that went with the height, a wide barrel torso, arms thicker than most legs. There was a volcano burning inside him that showed in lava sparks when he wasn't suppressing it. Every action he took had great force to it. Esbeth had ordered thinly sliced pork chops, just to see him work. He didn't use a meat slicer. Instead, he cut with a cleaver, with hard precise chops to the block that rattled the room. But Esbeth ended up with some of the thinnest, most cleanly sliced pork chops she'd ever seen.

"It must have taken a terrible brutish force to do that to Jake," Sue Belle said, and her voice wavered. They were identical to the words Deputy Bob had used. "I had to identify the body parts, you know."

They strolled for a while. Esbeth pumped her and got her version of the family struggles, all in spite of them each being nearly saints, to hear her tell it. When Esbeth begged off to leave, Sue Belle asked for a ride home.

"I was in an accident," she explained, nodding down at her arm in its sling. "Jake ran the wrecking yard, was gonna help me with my car." That started sniffles that erupted in another gush of tears, body-jerking good ones that made it hard for her to get into Esbeth's car. Once inside and two tissues later, she finally managed directions to her apartment and told Esbeth she was between husbands at the moment. The scoop Esbeth had gotten from Scottie was that she had had five husbands so far, was kind of on the revolving door plan. Esbeth gathered from him that Sue Belle was prone to wear them out.

They got to Sue Belle's place, a three-floor walk-up in a white wooden building. Of course she wanted to lean on Esbeth all the way up. But the poor thing, she was so weak and rattled Esbeth had to take the key out of her hand at the door and let her in.

The door swung open. "It's not much," she said, showing a delight in understatement Esbeth doubted she knew she had. The place wasn't tacky, no velvet Elvis painting able to shed tears. But Esbeth had always wondered where people bought those fuzzy dice that hung in cars. She bet Sue Belle knew where, though there were none in evidence. Everything, and there wasn't that much, was cheap. Clean and neatly spread in the corners of the room but sparse.

Sue Belle had wiped her face off in the car ride to her place, dabbing her tongue on a clean hankie Esbeth had in the car to rub away the smudged makeup, what folks used to call a spit bath. Now, in the light of her apartment, her face without makeup looked farm girl fresh, a few years showing but with the innocence of an adult who had either missed or was still living her childhood.

"Do you want a drink of water before you go?"

Esbeth didn't but wanted to see her kitchen, so she nodded. She managed a peek over Sue Belle's shoulder into her refrigerator as she swung it quickly open and closed. Little in there besides an open and sad-looking box of baking soda. Mother Hubbard would feel at home in Sue Belle's place. A nearly empty half gallon of Popov vodka sat by a glass on the kitchen table.

She gave Esbeth an embarrassed grin, the first smile Esbeth had seen so far, and led the way to the small living room. A row of unframed photos had been spread across a low table along the wall—the former husbands, Esbeth guessed. Two kids were in the last picture that finished the row.

"Them's the kids," Sue Belle said. They stay with their pa, Bill—no, Lennie." She shared an awkward giggle. Then she gave an equally realistic stretch. "I gotta get up early. The sheriff wants to see Jake's yard." Esbeth thought she meant a lawn until she remembered Jake worked in a wrecking yard. Sue Belle added another yawn. Esbeth took the hint and left.

Call her a soft touch, but Esbeth drove to the nearest grocery she knew of—open 24 hours, the sign said—and loaded up two bags of stuff she thought would be easy for Sue Belle to fix: soups, cans of tuna, fresh fruit, and vegetables. She regretted the cans and heavier stuff as she lugged them up the flights of stairs to Sue Belle's door. She stood there panting until she had her wind back then rang Sue Belle's bell and hustled down the stairs before she had to face Sue Belle accepting the groceries.

What the heck. The way she grew up, folks always rallied around with food at a death in someone's family.

Chapter 3: Junkyard Dog

After Esbeth got back to the car and took a few deep breaths, she realized she was just a couple of blocks from the family home, so she stopped off to pay her respects to Sadie. It had been a long day, and she was tuckered, but even old Sherlock never solved anything by sitting home on his duff.

Sadie answered the door looking like she carried more than a little of the world's woes on her back. She was the only one of them old enough for Esbeth to know well, for her to call Esbeth by name. There was a flicker of suspicion when she recognized Esbeth, but she let it fade away and asked Esbeth in for tea. Esbeth was not real surprised to find a big brooding fellow in a dark suit sitting on her couch. "This is Jeremy," she said and slipped into the kitchen to get another cup. The pot and a cup were in front of him on the couch. He didn't rise when Esbeth entered, still didn't until she walked all the way over to him, held out a hand.

He stood, sighed, and held out a hand, which Esbeth shook, though it surprised her. To look at him, you had to figure him for a weight lifter. He was tall with wide shoulders, a narrow waist, and had obvious muscle stacked all over him. Yet his handshake was clammy and limp like a quick visit to a fish market. Maybe it was the mortuary game that gave him that. Esbeth had heard that a lot of bodybuilders lifted weights to compensate for some insecurity. That could be it as well. He had another habit Esbeth found disconcerting, that of looking down then back up at you like you might have changed since he last looked. When he turned to fluff a cushion before easing back onto the couch, Esbeth thought his shoulders looked pinched from the back, the arms extending outward, not like a muscle-laden person's would but like someone carrying a lot of inner tension.

"It's all so very horrible, grisly," Sadie said when she'd poured tea into the cup she brought Esbeth. She plopped back into a favorite chair. "Who'd ever have thought one of my..." Her voice cracked, and she did not try to speak for a moment.

"Ain't you the one likes to solve..." she started when she could speak again.

"Aren't." Esbeth said it before she thought, caught the puckered and clenched mouth Jeremy gave her, the one you got when you corrected someone's grammar. But Sadie didn't mind, went on as if not interrupted. She had a fine soft southern voice, slurring over some words, shifting the emphasis on others.

Something Esbeth had noticed about people with heavy southern accents was that they seemed to enjoy hearing the sounds of the words that poured like syrup out of their mouths. They sometimes took longer to say things, repeat other things. Sadie was that way.

"What can you do?" she said. "No one gives you no instruction book on raising kids. Leastwise they didn't when I was rearing these. If Rufe'd been around, maybe things'd..." She gave Esbeth a sympathetic look. "I never took to seeing anyone after he walked out, kind of lost my taste for it. He was sitting here in this very chair, waitin' for dinner after comin' in from the wreckin' yard. The kids was fightin'. He just got up and walked out. Never saw him no more, nor heard from him again."

Jeremy looked on the verge of saying something but didn't.

"I don't know that I understand," Esbeth said. "But I can relate. I never had kids of my own, have kind of a short fuse around them. I hear that having them changes you, makes you more patient, but I've always suspected that it changes more for women than men."

"I hear you," she said. "They were a burden. But I loved 'em... all of 'em." That broke her up again.

Esbeth excused herself, left Sadie racked with jerking sobs on the chair. Jeremy showed Esbeth out, a shadow of a smirk behind the stern mask of his face. Esbeth had to confess that there was something about this man-boy she did not care for. To tell the truth, she looked for the same things in a man now as she did sixty years ago—decisiveness and confidence. That didn't mean cocky. It meant the opposite of confused, uncertain, or brash to overcompensate for insecurity. Not that she was on the prowl, now or then. But some of the measures of men still held. Jeremy had none of the traits she admired, but he thought he did.

"Sheriff Danvers tells us that what happened to Jake took place two days ago, Wednesday," he said once the door had closed and the two of them stood alone on the porch. "I was here with Mom all day. I don't get anything out of it either. The yard'll go to Sue Belle to sell for what she can get, and she's welcome to it. She and Jake were always so damned close."

"Tarnation," Esbeth said, something that no real old person would say but she did just to see young folks' eyes bulge. He just stared at her with his mortuary look, full of plastic flower sadness. She was weighing what he'd said like she did all volunteered alibis.

Well, what a fine kettle of fish. She stewed on what little she had so far on the way home. She was asleep almost as soon as she plopped on the old bed at home that night. She was too pooped for her usual bat-tle with insomnia, for which she usually drank a glass of wine. It didn't help her sleep, but she minded being up less.

The next morning, before daylight, she drove over to the Marston wrecking yard, so early the fellows who had worked for Jake weren't even there yet. The place had a high chain-link fence and the usual un-fed dog that barked its Doberman head off until she tossed the meat she'd brought over the fence. That old mutt was licking her hand be-tween the links while she picked at the lock and slipped inside for a look. Don't let anyone tell you that a schoolteacher can't learn any new tricks in forty years of dealing with teenagers. She'd locked herself out of enough places and had to open enough other locks the kids put on things to learn to pick some of the best. She'd even gotten herself a lockpick set from one of her former students who was now holding up the inner walls of one of our sturdier institutions.

She had a look around, even looked over Sue Belle's car, still parked on the lot waiting for Jake to fix it. Esbeth had looked up the accident report. Sue Belle claimed to have hydroplaned off the street into a tree. But Esbeth suspected that there was more liquid in Sue Belle than on the street. The right front end was smashed, the steering wheel pressed back where it had broken her arm. But Esbeth supposed someone could fix it if they knew what they were doing and had a wrecking yard full of parts to work with.

A wrecking yard was a man kind of a place, she guessed—full of tools, grease, and huge machines for cutting or mashing cars. This one had more wrecked cars, stacks of tires, and piles of salvaged parts than she cared to ever see again soon. Jake's yard was made eerier by the gathering threads of light from the creeping dawn that had to weasel its way through scattered dark clouds. She glanced up at one point in one of those short bursts of flickering dim light to glance east, see how much time she had left. She rocked back on her heels when she realized she was looking at the horizon through the jaws of a machine the size, shape, and disposition of a *Tyrannosaurus rex*'s head. Once her heart had settled back into a mere semi-frantic downhill gallop, she flipped on the hand-flash she carried and gave it the going-over she had all the massive gadgets. She could imagine that by day some of these machines were as noisy and smelly as they were repulsive to look at in the half light. She tried to envision a day spent in the sun, dust, grime, stink, and racket of all of these going at once. That must have been why they called it work.

An hour or so later, the sun was up far enough for her to figure she had better get out of there before the help arrived. But just as she got up to the front gate, the dog clicking along beside her like a K-9 trooper, a sheriff's car pulled up. Danvers himself was in there, and Bob, someone else as well. Well, that torched it. She was not as spry as she used to be. There was no place to hide. She stood out in the open and couldn't have run for it if she'd been able.

Chapter 4: Law and Older

Sheriff Danvers was out of his door, yelling, "Esbeth Walters. Is that you?"

The dog charged the fence, started barking frantically, snarling and snapping. Bob got out the other door. "Yep. It's her. Want me to...?" All this above the dog's yapping.

"Come here," she yelled. The dog did. "Sit." It did. She wished she had a picture of the expressions on their faces, or on Sue Belle's as she got out of the car as well.

"Luke and Juan ain't here yet," she said. Her face looked like she'd been up crying or drinking most of the night, maybe both.

Esbeth went to the gate, let herself out, and slid the lock back into place but didn't close it.

"I thought I told you..." Bob started, more in his own defense than to chastise Esbeth.

"Well, Miss Nosy Parker," Danvers put it nicely, "you solve this case too?" His tone was more sententious than sarcastic. His opponent last election had called Danvers "Mr. S," for "snide, snotty, surly, and snarly." But Danvers had held his office.

"Lord knows we have enough likely suspects this time. Maybe even Rufus came back to..."

"Don't say that 'bout Daddy," Sue Belle snapped.

Bob, who was a lot sharper than he let on, was watching Esbeth's face, had seen something there.

"Still trying to teach us our jobs? Long as you were a schoolteacher, Esbeth," Danvers said, "you must've learned that you can lead a horse to water, but you can't make it drink." He laughed, but Bob didn't join him.

"I did learn," Esbeth said, "that now and again you can make a horse thirsty, though."

"Should we round anyone up?" Danvers said. Esbeth was almost to them. "Who did it?"

"Yeah, who?" Bob echoed, only not with the salt-in-the-wound laughter the sheriff was sharing.

"You don't have to round anyone up," Esbeth said, staring at Sue Belle.

Danvers stared at Esbeth, didn't see Sue Belle spin on him and take off running. But Bob was already moving and caught her only a dozen steps from the cruiser. Good thing, too, because Esbeth's days of running were twenty years past.

If she didn't feel so bone weary and lousy in general, she would have enjoyed the look on Danvers's face more as it swung from the kicking and screaming Sue Belle back to Esbeth. "Well, I'll be..."

Esbeth did humble well. After they booked Sue Belle and Esbeth had finished her statement, Danvers came over to her with the same hangdog look he'd worn after the Fergusson case. Esbeth didn't want to be too hard on someone no higher up on the food chain than he was.

"You'd have gotten it, Sheriff, as soon as you looked over that big crushing machine in there. They must have been fooling around in the wrecking yard about getting her car back together, him leaning where he shouldn't have been when it hit her to throw the switch on the damned thing. It's been hosed off. But enough blood's still on it for a good forensics crew to work with. I don't know why she chopped up the rest of him and spread him around town like that unless she was trying to divert the suspicion."

"I had Ged Svenson figured for it sure," Danvers admitted, his face settling into jowls as he sank back in his chair. "He had the brute strength, I figured, and had probably been stewing on that feud business for years."

"He cut some of the cleanest chops you ever saw for me with a cleaver," Esbeth said. "If he'd done it, the severed edges would have been a whole lot neater."

"I liked the brother Jeremy for it," Bob Clanton said as he came in and plopped down in the wooden chair beside Esbeth.

"I wish it had been him," she admitted. "But he didn't have the real spine for it. If you were ever drowning, he'd be the guy to throw you both ends of the rope. But he wouldn't start anything. Sue Belle was the person of action among them. She was the one who put in the fake obituary that time, and she had the most to gain by Jake's death."

"She seemed so frail, one arm in a sling like that," Bob said. "And I thought she really loved Jake."

"I think she did," Esbeth said. "But she was down to nothing. I couldn't check through the bank, but I could go through the credit union. Her plastic was run out to the edges, and she didn't act like someone with a purse full of cash. Her infidelities kept her from the kind of alimony she would have liked."

"Yeah," Danvers agreed. "When you been in more laps than a napkin..." He stopped himself when he caught Esbeth's expression. He shifted gears. "I've got to hand it to you, with my thanks of course. Though we were on our way to the yard with her to look around, and we might have found what you did, since you had more reason to be looking for it. But we might have missed it as well." It was hard for him to manage, and Bob seemed to get a lot of pleasure from hearing him struggle.

The police band radio saved Danvers more embarrassment. It crackled to life with, "We've got three bodies here so far and are still counting." They both leaped to their feet. Esbeth followed more slowly.

The cruiser with both of them in it was peeling out of the lot on two tires as she made her tired way to her car. Well, nothing ever happened around there, and it was happening again.

Chapter 5: Murder at the Tupperware Party

"What're you in for?" the woman in the short leather skirt and fishnet stockings asked Esbeth. She leaned her back against the bars of the cell door, one foot on the corner of the steel cot built into the block wall. She picked at a gap in her teeth with a false fingernail long enough for peeling peaches.

Now that was one question you didn't expect to hear when you were seventy-some years old and in the prime of old maidness, as Esbeth was while the 1980s were rolling merrily along. In all her time on the planet, she thought she'd heard all the stinger lines, ranging from "Did you used to be pretty?" to the all-time dancing favorite, "You don't sweat much for a fat girl."

But back a handful of hours ago, when Blanche Obbaggabidge had keeled over deader than a bent grape during the *hors d'oeuvre* portion of a Tupperware confab at Esbeth's house, she hadn't expected to be the one fingered for the crime.

"Murder," Esbeth said. That shut the street trooper up. She pushed away from the bars and went over to sit on the far end of her cot, giving Esbeth occasional peeks of disbelief. So Esbeth added, "I'd lose that blouse, too, if I were you. It does you no justice, makes you look cheap."

"Well, I never."

"You have now, sister." Esbeth was not really as tough as she sounded, looked more like she ought to be on a rocker knitting than standing restless in a holding cell. But she was just scared enough being in jail for the first time in her life to try to assert herself. She'd watched too much television probably. The 1980s were rolling along, and she hoped to be out in time to enjoy the turn of the century.

Just when she was needing it most, the steel door at the front clanged open, and a friendly face came down the hallway. Deputy Bob Clanton carried a brown shopping bag. He was glancing up and down the hallway as he came to her cell door, and she could swear he was blushing at seeing Esbeth behind bars. He had been one of her pupils when she taught school math back a long time ago—she believed dinosaurs still freely roamed the earth in those days.

"How's the food?" he said, glancing down at her untouched tray.

"Good as what you'd get on an airplane, I suppose. Isn't it a marvel how they can press cardboard into the shape of, say, shrimp scampi?"

"I'm sorry about all this," he said, actually lowering his head for a moment. When he looked up, he grinned. "I brought you something, though." He reached into his bag and brought out a red-and-white-striped box. The smell of chicken wafted through the bars. He held the box out to her, "Don't pick the lock or anything with the bones, or Danvers'll be all over me."

"Ah," Esbeth said as she pulled the box between the bars, "if the sheriff were only as human as you, I wouldn't be in here."

"It won't be much longer probably. The others are coming in for their polygraphs. You've already had yours. Just be glad you're not down in the men's bullpen with some guy in for worrying sheep."

"Got to count the small blessings," Esbeth agreed. But he had already turned and was clicking back toward the one door out of the place.

Not twenty minutes later the door banged open again. Bob Clanton was back, with Scottie in tow this time, Scottie's hand rising restlessly toward the pack of cigarettes in his pocket, dropping again. Scottie was a photographer at the local *Daily Planet*. He was doing his best to suppress a smile as he peered through the bars where Esbeth and her cellmate were dining in style, throwing the bones on the floor. For her age, Esbeth gave less of a hoot about low-fat, low-cholesterol than she should.

Scottie was giving the hairy eyeball to the woman beside Esbeth. "LaToya," Esbeth said, "meet Scottie."

"Pleased, I'm sure," she said, her little finger curled in the air, her teeth chonked back into the flesh of a drumstick she held with both hands.

"What're you in for?" Scottie asked her.

She was busy chewing, so Esbeth answered for her. "Standing too close to the curb, I think. Are you here to bail me or to build a relationship?"

"The D.A. laughed the charge down to material witness," he said. "I doubt I could've scraped up the scratch for the other charge if they'd have had enough to make it stick."

Esbeth was ushered out of her cell, led down the long hallway, and checked in with the desk sergeant. She got her purse and other stuff from the manila envelope and started for the exit from the sheriff's office.

"Isn't that ol' Cecil over there?" Scottie asked.

"It sure is." Cecil was Blanche's husband—the late Blanche, Esbeth guessed it was. "He's coming out of the room where I had my polygraph session," she told Scottie.

"How'd you do?"

"You should'a seen that needle dance when they asked my age."

Cecil turned the wrong way, stood staring with a puzzled look at a wall, wondering maybe where the door had gone. Esbeth hated to say the *A* word, but some folks thought Cecil had more than a touch of Alzheimer's.

"This way," Scottie hollered over to him. He waved toward the door where they were headed. Much as Esbeth felt sorry for Cecil, she flinched when he started over toward them. At one time or another, he had hit on every one of Blanche's friends. Esbeth didn't know that anything ever came of it, or that he was even able to help himself.

He tottered toward the door alongside them. "You're lookin' fine, Esbeth," he said. "Want to go somewheres and rub the bacon?"

"Cecil, you're all of ninety-four," Esbeth snapped. "You've had it."

"Oh," he said, the puzzled look coming back over his face. "How was I?"

Scottie held the door open and reached for his pack of Chesterfields with his other hand. He was struggling to keep back a grin. The sun hammered down on them. It seemed unusually bright out, the clear sky not helping. The temperature was somewhere over a hundred. But she didn't mind. It felt good to be outside.

Smoke billowed around Scottie's head. Cecil stood there, a blank look carved into his long wrinkled pan, his big ears sticking out like radar hooked to some other planet. He looked kind of sad, like that *American Gothic* painting only without the pitchfork or the woman. Thinking about Blanche being dead washed all over Esbeth again. It pepped her a bit, made her eager to do something about it.

"Now, Esbeth," Scottie said, must have seen the glitter in her eyes, a look he'd seen before. Esbeth could see apprehension sliding across his mug. "You've kicked plenty of sand in Danvers's face before. Hadn't you better leave this for him to solve this time." He'd been the one, after all, to take her picture for the paper. But this time the case was too close to home for her to leave alone.

"What've your journalistic ears picked up so far?" she pressed. She stood still, letting the hot Texas sun beat down on them, warm up her jail-cooled old bones. Scottie was a good newshound, though he'd be the last to admit it. He was always grousing about being bogged down taking pictures of some baby parade or something, but his seasoned nose twitched at a scoop the way she couldn't help meddling in cases others might leave unsolved.

"I hear all the others passed their polygraphs, same as you."

"Now if I could just pin down which one at the party is the biggest liar." The Q&A inside had spent a lot of time on poison, motive, and opportunity. Sheriff Danvers must have figured someone there had slipped Blanche the fatal dose, and for once Esbeth agreed with him.

"If we had ham, we could have ham and eggs," Scottie said, "if we had eggs."

Esbeth gave him the lowered brow look she saved to settle down his attempts at wit. Once he had that little limp analogy out of his system maybe they could get down to business.

"I want to go to the morgue." She realized as soon as she'd said it that Cecil was still standing by them, might have taken that wrong. But he gazed out into the passing traffic, looking like both oars weren't in the water.

What Esbeth had meant was the newspaper morgue. Scottie knew that. It was where she could get background on the guests to her Tupperware debacle she did not have prior to hosting a murder.

First, they got Cecil loaded into Roy's cab. Esbeth was giving the driver directions to Cecil's place when Cecil's head snapped to her, some bulb in his head having gone off, "Hey, Esbeth, you mess around detecting stuff, solved a couple of hot ones. Think you can see what happened to Blanche?"

As he said it, the realization swept over his face that she was gone. He dissolved into a blubbering spell. That was the thing about the big *A*. Sometimes he had spells of lucidity. They came and went, mostly went. But there was no counting on him for any kind of a stretch. Esbeth finished giving directions to the driver and paid him in advance, just in case Cecil wasn't up to it or had forgotten money.

Esbeth tagged along with the grumping Scottie as they went to the newspaper office. A few of the other newshawks were at their desks, pecking at stories and items. The big rush for today's deadline was past. None of them paid Esbeth much mind, even though her accoutrement was a bit wrinkled and worn from having spent the night in the hoosegow. Scottie pulled the morgue files she asked for and let her sit at his desk and poke through them, making a few notes.

He leaned over her shoulder, added clouds of Chesterfield smoke to the confusion she already had as she checked off the names on her guest list.

"Why did *you* have a Tupperware party in the first place?" he asked, waving away part of the smoke he was generating. "That's not your usual thing. You usually do fine staying off by yourself with your crossword puzzles or whatever."

"Even lone wolves get a little lonely sometimes."

Scottie tilted his head, let one eyebrow arch a bit, the eye beneath it squinting against the smoke.

He began to choke. Esbeth was about to say that it served him right, that he ought to give up the coffin nails. But it was not her style to judge others or to bug them about their habits.

"I was just trying to picture you," he said, when his pipes worked again, "up on some rock with the moon behind you, your head pitched back in a howl."

Chapter 6: So No One Bought Any Tupperware?

In a true journalistic segue, Scottie asked, "Who asked you to host the party, anyway?"

"Blanche," Esbeth said. "The soiree was supposed to be at her place, but the termite folks were swarming through her place like Union troops through Atlanta."

"Quite a racy list," Scottie said, poking at her notes. "Anyone in this bunch born in this century or the previous?"

There were Blanche and Cecil, Lucy Armstrong, Mel and Irma Finch, and Melissa Prentice. Melissa was only fifty-five, though she claimed to be in her forties. But Esbeth didn't want to knock Scottie off his soapbox by pointing out what an infant Melissa was.

"Who you going to start on first?"

"Lucy, I think," Esbeth said. "She knows poisons."

"You kidding?

"I guess you've never tasted her cooking. Besides, she brought most of the food. Why don't you be a dear and see what you can dig up from forensics for me?"

But he was spared getting off his duff by a young cub of a reporter hustling in from outside, sweat glistening on his forehead and his shirt soaked through in spots. It had been a long while since Scottie had hustled like that, or needed to.

"Scott," the kid yelled, "this Tupperware caper's turning into a real hoot. The wire services are all over it, calling it a real whodunit. You're tight with that old coot who threw the thing, aren't you? Think you could...?" He screeched to a halt as he got close enough to see Esbeth sitting in Scottie's command module and Scottie at her shoulder.

"Why don't you ask the old coot herself?" Scottie said.

"Sorry about that, ma'am."

"You're gonna be sorry, you call me ma'am again," Esbeth said.

"It's all right, Trent," Scottie said to calm him. "She's helping me with the story."

"What really went on over there?" The kid recovered well, the red seeping back out of his face as he tugged a chair closer and sat, his pad out.

"Mostly it was us ex-schoolteachers jawing about that poll that was just published, the one that said folks respected elementary and high school teachers, along with college professors the most, while they distrusted lawyers and reporters. Called you guys bottom-feeders."

"I guess I had that coming," Trent said. "Now, can you give me any of the dirt of what went on over there?"

Esbeth had to admire his sticking to his job. She glanced at Scottie. He nodded, which vouched for the cub reporter in a way the kid wouldn't know for a few years.

"We had just passed the first tray of *hors d'oeuvres*," Esbeth said, "calves' liver wrapped in bacon and coconut shrimp. Lucy Armstrong had made them, and you know she wins a prize at nearly every state fair—that is, until Blanche scooped her the past two years. Blanche skipped on the food, was beefing about spending the morning in the dentist's chair getting a minor scaling. But the rest of us figured she was giving Lucy a bit of a snub. All of us had iced tea, except Melissa Prentice, who had coffee. Imagine, a hundred degrees outside and she has coffee. There's a bit of Yankee left in that woman, I can tell you."

Trent was scribbling away on his notepad. He looked up. "Just a little under-the-surface cat-fight tension, huh? But no real arguments?"

"No."

"Then what?"

"Blanche turned real pale. Her face got stiff, the eyes staring, then her head lowered, like she couldn't lift it. Her skin started turning kind of blue. Then she keeled over into the *hors d'oevre* tray. Lucy popped up, started to say she might have done it on purpose. But Blanche was in a dead faint. She was dead before the EMS vehicle got there."

"So, no one bought any Tupperware, huh?"

"Watch your back with Danvers," Scottie unnecessarily warned Esbeth as he drove her back to her place, "remember that he got into law enforcement because it's a business where the customer is usually wrong."

"Yeah, yeah, yeah." Esbeth waved him off and bustled inside. She wanted to see the folks from the party before they were talked to death by the law and journalists. She also wanted to clean up the house, and it needed a quick lick. She had got to admit that a little power nap was sounding good right then, but she didn't even glance at the sofa or the bed as she quickly changed and took off again.

Lucy Armstrong's place was closest to hers, just a block and a half away. So she hiked the distance, got in a little post-jail exercise. Besides, she wanted to start with her anyway, get her over with, to tell the truth.

Lucy sat on her porch swing, snapping the widespread pages of the newspaper held in front of her as far as her arms could reach. She wore black, in deference to Blanche, and looked not a little like a buzzard hovering over a carcass. Her white hair was in a tight bun. Her beak swung up, and she glared as Esbeth hiked up her sidewalk toward her.

"Thought you were in jail," she said. "I'd thrown in the trowel on you. Why'd they arrest you in the first place? What're you doing out?" Her flinty black eyes flicked up and down Esbeth, but she didn't invite her out of the sun up onto the porch or get her a lemonade or anything.

Esbeth answered her questions in order. "Because the party was at my place and I'd mixed the drinks, the iced tea, and coffee. They seem to think she drank some poison. I'm out because I didn't do it."

"Humpf," she said. "And you're poking around 'cause you think there's something rotten in Detroit."

"Probably is, but that has nothing to do with this case."

"Well, why're you always the one who pokes around, won't let up 'til the last dog has sung."

"It happened at my house," Esbeth said. "That upsets my sensibilities." She got back to it. "You're sure there was nothing in the food?"

"Of course there wasn't. Are you sure there even *was* any poison? Seems far-fetched to me. When they told me Blanche was actually dead, you could have knocked me into a crocked hat."

For some reason, talking with Lucy was always fingernails on a chalkboard for Esbeth, even when she was, as she had put it in the past, feeling knobbier than Nebuchadnezzar. She was Esbeth's age, had a lot of firm ideas, one of them being that Esbeth ought to act her age and sit around, more like her. Esbeth doubted she would get much from her but asked anyway. "You see anyone slip anything into the drinks?"

Lucy's head rocked back, aghast at the idea. As those Zen folks said, sometimes no answer *was* an answer. Esbeth bet the officers had fun administering the polygraph test to her.

"Your tea was awful bitter. I noticed you wasn't drinking any. If poor Blanche hadn't just come from the dentist, maybe she wouldn't've drank as much as she did."

"You won almost every state fair ribbon there is for your recipes until the past two years. Then Blanche won two years straight. I saw a clipping where you claimed she'd stolen your recipes to win. Is there anything to that?"

"How could you bring that up now? We'd settled all that. It's so much water under the bridge now. We were best friends again, or she wouldn't have invited me. It was all the bilk of human kindness between us again."

Esbeth shifted gears, "Did Cecil ever make a pass at you?"

Well, that old biddy. She blushed and lowered her head, raised it, sheepish before snapping back into character. "Needless to say, I let him know he was casting his burls before twine."

Even though she was standing out in the sun, that one sent a chilly shudder through Esbeth. She couldn't tell whether Lucy twisted clichés into knots like that on purpose or because she couldn't help herself. In either case, she'd had enough of a dose for now.

Esbeth hiked back to the street and over to her own place, changed out of her sweaty dress, and took a quick dip in a cool tub of water before gearing up again and heading over to Melissa Prentice's place by car.

Chapter 7: Boil, Boil, Poison, and Trouble

Melissa Prentice lived way on the other side of town. Esbeth could swear that every other street was torn up with one kind of construction or another. In the stop-and-go traffic, she had a chance to think while her car fought to keep from overheating. She clicked off what she had so far. There was bug poison at Blanche's house. She'd probably had gas or novocaine at the dentist's office. Esbeth had mixed the iced tea and coffee, knew there was nothing in that when she'd handed the tray to Cecil. Lucy had made the food. Forensics would know more about that. Lucy had skirted that stolen recipe issue in a pretty glib fashion. Esbeth swung the car over into the shady side of a convenience store, dialed Scottie while she gave the car a chance to cool.

He wasn't at his desk, so she asked for Trent. His eager voice came on. "Scottie's over with Danvers. It sounded like he was on to something."

"Did they get anything solid from forensics?"

"Yeah," Trent said. "Looks like curare all right. Fits with the symptoms. I'm doing the digging on that. I'm surprised at all the places you can get it. Physicians use it a lot, some as a muscle relaxant before surgery because it reduces the anesthesia the patient'll need. Some use it to relieve spastic paralysis. Others use it as an anticonvulsant, for dealing with, say, tetanus. The Latinate handle of the stuff used is *Chododendron tomentosum*. That's opposed to *Stychnos toxifera*. But there are half a dozen trade names for it I've found so far. Did you know...?"

"Sounds like you're going to be quite a reporter," Esbeth wedged in. A trickle of sweat had started down her back. She shivered, though she could see hazy waves of heat rising from the asphalt near her.

"Let me know if you hear anything from those at the party. Scottie said that you'd be sticking your... that you'd be asking them some questions."

"I'll keep you posted."

"Hey, Esbeth?" She caught his voice as she was hanging up, drew the receiver back to her ear. "Poisonings aren't all that common. In fact, this is the first one like this in years. It'd be a real scoop for me."

"Okay, kid," Esbeth said. "Now I've got to go before I melt like a Popsicle."

Melissa Prentice lived in a condo along a second-rate golf course. Jets from the nearby airport lifted noisily overhead. But the grounds were neat and well-kept, made for a nice lawn and view. Esbeth wondered who had bought her the condo. The morgue file on her noted only that she had been Mel Finch's secretary until he retired from his medical supply business. Cecil had been his regular accountant all those years, which was the connection that tied them all together.

The door opened, and Melissa peered out, blinking against the sun. "Why, come on in, Esbeth. I'm so glad they let you out. I knew that you'd never..."

Esbeth was only half listening to her cheerful bubbling as Melissa ushered her through her place to the breakfast nook. She was wearing a multicolored house dress that was the equivalent of a Hawaiian shirt. Well, Esbeth thought, welcome to the colorized version of life. It was an odd time of life for someone like Esbeth when she realized that the vamps in her circle were whippersnappers in their fifties.

"You want some coffee? I just made a fresh pot."

Esbeth's original thought had been that whatever poison had been used would be one that reacted to, say, heat. But that came from reading mysteries. The curare finding knocked all that out.

"It's my real vice," she said as she poured cups for them, "my picker-upper. I buy the beans special. You should take some of mine home. I'm not being critical, but yours is kind of strong. You don't get that New Orleans kind with chicory in it, do you?"

Esbeth felt sensitive about her hospitality right then, must have just nodded. She did notice that even in the breakfast nook, Melissa had positioned them so that Esbeth was in the direct light coming in from the windows. Melissa had a little shadow going for her. Even though she was quite a bit younger than Esbeth, she had her vanity. Her hair was naturally blond, or had been—touched up, Esbeth supposed. It was cut in a Doris Day kind of bowl but did nothing for the way gravity was starting to be cruel to her cheeks. At Esbeth's age, Melissa was going to have jowls. As it was, her cheeks had begun to droop, sagging down toward the beginning of a double chin.

"You talk to any of the others?"

"Just Lucy."

"That woman. She wears me down listening to her. She got going one day talking about Jason and his golden fleas. Can you imagine?"

Melissa's eyes were pale blue but had a sultry cast to them. Esbeth could see why older guys still went for her. She dressed well, didn't threaten with her intelligence, had worked on the total package. Still, all those years of living as she had did not help her reputation much. If Esbeth had been more of the butt-in type, she would have told Melissa long ago that dating men a platoon at a time was no one's idea of platonic love.

Melissa plowed along with her animated conversation for a while before Esbeth brought up Blanche as a topic.

"No. I didn't see anyone mess with the food or the beverages. I answered all that for those men at the sheriff's department. If you lived closer in town, we would have at least been dealing with city policemen. They're much more handsome. That Danvers is so serious."

Esbeth nodded. "For him, detective work must seem to be the constant unfolding of miscalculations." She shifted gears. "Did Cecil ever hit on you?"

"Did he? Well, who hasn't? But that poor man was so... so... Well, there was just no interest for me."

"I wouldn't normally pry," Esbeth said, lifting her cup to drain the last of the cool coffee, "except there's a death involved. Were you and Mel ever... close?"

"*Were* we? I don't mind telling you, Esbeth, we were more than close. He met Irma a long time back, said that if only he'd met me first. He was ready to leave her a couple of times for me, but I was the one who wouldn't let him. He's the kind of guy that got all excited about nothing then married her. But I knew I had his interest much better when I was just a sideline for him."

Melissa poured Esbeth more coffee, and she grabbed for it. Esbeth felt a sudden coolness she wanted to warm up. She tried hard *not* to picture them together—intimate, all that. She'd never been in a situation like that with a boss, didn't want to judge Melissa. But it was a struggle.

"I don't think old Cecil would have ever gotten as worked up as he did if Mel hadn't said something to him at one time or another. You know how men are, bragging and all."

Esbeth didn't, nor did she really want to. But it was useful information.

Chapter 8: The Missing Motive

Easing out of the air conditioning into the midday heat, Esbeth high-stepped it to her car and got the air on there. If it wasn't for iced tea and air conditioning, most folks couldn't even live in Texas. But the heat felt kind of good, seared away some of the contact she'd had with Melissa, or Muffy, as she had said Mel liked to call her. Esbeth was beginning to realize why she liked to spend so much time alone.

Esbeth was heading for Mel and Irma Finch's, her last stop, when she thought she'd pop in on Cecil. He lived just half a block from them, and she wasn't sure he would be getting along all that well all by himself. In spite of the squabbles he sometimes had with Blanche, she was more than a bit of the glue that held him together. He'd been revolving in and out of lucidity when last Esbeth had seen him. The impact of Blanche's death had to be hitting him hard by now.

A sheriff's car was parked along the curb in front of the house Blanche and Cecil had shared. Danvers himself came out, leading Cecil toward the cruiser. Deputy Bob Clanton and Scottie were in the small parade.

"You booking him?" she asked Danvers.

He just scowled at her, went around, and got into the driver's side while Bob led Cecil to the back seat. Danvers muttered to himself.

"What'd he say?" Esbeth asked Scottie. "My ears aren't as good as I'd like."

"Something about detective work, like prostitution, being ruined by amateurs," Scottie grinned. "What're you here for?"

"On my way to see the Finches, wanted to check on Cec first." Cecil stood by the car in the sun, his cheeks sparkling where tears were quietly trickling down them. He stared ahead, not seeming to recognize Esbeth or have a clue what was happening to him.

"Looks like we got our man this time," Bob Clanton said to me, pressing down on Cecil's head as he lowered him into the back seat. "Irma Finch saw him putting something in the drinks. You're lucky all of you weren't killed. With his memory, he's the only one of you could have sailed through the polygraph tests too."

"Danvers was leaning at first toward Mel," Scottie said, "because of the medical supply business."

"You know what you're missing?" Esbeth asked.

"What?" Bob wanted not to ask but couldn't help himself.

"Motive," Esbeth said.

"Lots of men dust off their wives after years of living together," Bob said but did not sound all that convinced in this case.

"Not this one." Esbeth glanced from Bob to Scottie, back again. "Do you think you can keep Danvers here until I talk with the Finches?"

"What are you...?"

Scottie interrupted Clanton. "Give it a shot, Esbeth. But don't be wrong." He looked at her, into her, knew she wasn't just messing around. Bob gave her the hangdog look he had last time when he knew she was going to prove the sheriff wrong, make life hell for him in the department.

Esbeth walked down to the Finch house, came back in less than five minutes with Mel and Irma in tow. Danvers was standing by his door, fuming.

"I don't see why we should...?" Mel was saying.

"For heaven's sake, Mel," Irma said, "the man and you were thick as thieves all those years. The least you could do is..."

Mel looked part bulldog, reminded Esbeth of the fellow who said his dog was part bull, had cost him a thousand. "What part's bull?" someone had asked him. "The part about the thousand dollars," he said.

Of all of their little circle, Mel was the one who should have been best prepared for retirement living, all those years of hustling medical supplies. But his shirt was frayed at the sleeves, and Esbeth had heard Irma talk of mending, pinching pennies to get by. Esbeth had wondered where some of the money had gone. According to the clippings in his file, Mel had made a tidy bundle when he sold his business when he retired. So far, it looked like Melissa was living better than him.

Cecil stared out the back window of the cruiser, his eyes connecting to things this time. Bob had rolled the window halfway down while they had sat in the heat and waited. "Esbeth," he boomed from the back seat, "did you find out anything about…?"

"Oh, shut him up," Danvers snapped at Bob.

"I think you should listen to him," Esbeth said with enough quiet authority to snap Danvers's head toward her. "When he's on the beam like now, he might be able to tell you a thing or two, like how he got the stuff from Mel, who probably told him it was *Cantharis vericatoria*, or Spanish fly."

"An orgy," Cecil said. "We was supposed to…"

Irma jumped forward, was all over Esbeth the way a lifetime mate would do. She stepped close, leaned forward into Esbeth's space, and yelled, "Why in God's green earth would Mel…?"

"To get Melissa Prentice off his back. They'd had an affair for years. He probably paid for that condo of hers, was still paying. But on a retirement income, he had less to share than before, wasn't getting any of the benefits either. I figure it was pretty close to blackmail."

Irma's mouth dropped open wide then snapped shut. She spun to Mel, who took an inadvertent step backward, bumping into Bob Clanton. "Say it's not… Say something. Just say something. Anything."

"Melissa had said no to Cecil," Esbeth said, "as so many women have." Cecil nodded there in the back seat of the cruiser. "He thought this was a way to turn her on. I figure we all drank some of the curare. But the only one it affected was Blanche because her gums were all raw from being at the dentist. Curare has to get into the bloodstream to work, doesn't have any effect just being swallowed. Mel must have been mixed up on that, thought it would break down in a hot drink, knew as only he could that Melissa was a hot coffee drinker, even in the middle of summer."

Scottie and Bob both had their hands full then holding Irma back from Mel. He seemed almost to welcome being put into the back of the sheriff's car with Cecil. They would have to take Cecil back down for a new statement. But they would have to wait for one of his lucid spells. For the moment, he was occupied, as the cruiser fired up and began to pull away, with staring out the window. Irma sat in the grass of Cecil and Blanche's lawn, crying and pounding the earth. Scottie stood beside her, staring at Esbeth. Cecil's eyes were on Irma's legs, where her skirt had ridden up. He was ogling her, varicose veins and all, as the car slowly pulled away.

"Heaven help me if I ever get old," Esbeth muttered under her breath.

Scottie's keen ears caught her, though. "Oh, I wouldn't worry about that. I'm pretty sure everyone will hear your tires squealing at the turn of the century."

Chapter 9: Stop on a Mime

Esbeth Walters sat at a table in the warm sun outside the Asian Food Market in Austin, in Stonewall Jackson Park, one of her favorite places to relax and do a little people watching while filling in a crossword in the folded paper in front of her. The breeze tugged at the corner of the paper, the wind warm enough to feel just a little tired. Some people nibble at a newspaper; Esbeth had devoured hers from one end to the other and was now finishing it off by doing the puzzle. Few people got as much from a newspaper as she did. A number of the other patrons of the market or park sat at the tables with umbrellas, deferring to a sun that had already pushed the thermometer into the 80s and looked like it would keep pushing. Esbeth liked the sun. As a retired school math teacher and a youngish 64, she savored the sauna qualities of sitting and sweating, the kind of exercise program a lizard might favor.

She filled in the last box, a trickle of moisture running down her temple, and considered going over to the market for a lemon squash, their old-world way of saying lemonade, and a small squid and seaweed salad. Chopsticks, of course. But she'd have to run the gauntlet. To her left a number of moms and tots made squealing use of a playground full of slides, swings, big brightly colored plastic tubes, wooden towers, and monkey bars. What child wouldn't enjoy that, and have to scream while doing so?

To her right, small semicircles of stone seats set into the dirt so long ago that grass had grown around them, rose in a progressive set upward on the hill that allowed music groups and summer theater troupes to perform in the open space before them. At the moment a mime held court there, a juggler having had his turn earlier and passed the hat and left. People were laughing at the mime's antics, but Esbeth wasn't one of them. Mimes were too much like clowns, and she was one of those few people who had experienced a scare from a clown as a child and thought people with those kinds of looks could and should rightly be weaponized and used overseas. In short, she did not like clowns or mimes. Especially mimes who mocked.

Sure enough, as she sought to make a discreet pass along the far playground side of the open space, this one spotted her and came up behind her and began to imitate her walk. Nothing could have irked her more. The people in the sprinkling of an audience didn't help by laughing hysterically. Esbeth had a build that had fought its battles with gravity and food. As a result, most of her was closer to the ground than not. She cast what some called a firm shadow, was at the very least pear-shaped. The mime had squatted low and waddled behind her, rear end thrust out far. She saw their shadows and guessed why some of the spectators were laughing so hard they might hurt themselves.

"Stop it," she hissed. "You make me look like a Hottentot." Then she realized he was probably one of the many who had neither read *National Geographic* nor knew a Hottentot from a Zulu. Still, his actions were disrespectful to the max.

She considered whirling and giving him a piece of her mind, as if she could spare it, when a car on the street ahead caught her attention. It was coming down the street very fast and swerved to hop over the curb and pass over the grass boulevard and sidewalk and now came straight at her. The car was unmistakably a red DeSoto sedan, 1960 model, one she would be hard-pressed not to know, since her grandfather's last car had been the same year and model, except his had been more of a robin's-egg blue.

Little time to think and reflect on that now. Despite her build, she could still be quick when circumstances called for it, and these did. She ran and dove, rolling in a tumble that was going to leave her a mass of skid marks tomorrow. She ended her roll on her elbows and looked back. The mime had not been so quick, or lucky. He sailed through the air and landed on the flat concrete surface. The car came to a skidding stop on top of him, one tire turning him into a biological speed bump in the process.

Whoever drove the car was out the driver's door and off and running away to the other side. Esbeth couldn't see anything except dark pants and black shoes as the person ran. The people on both sides, those being entertained by the mime and the children and their mothers on the other side all broke into a communal wave of screams, some repeating cries again and again. This was nothing a mother wanted a child to see.

Even Esbeth, who admitted to being fond of neither clowns nor mimes, could tell this one wasn't going to be mocking anyone again soon, or ever.

"**D**id you get the names and addresses of all the people in the audience and the moms in the play area?" Esbeth sat on the back of the EMS vehicle while a handsome young EMS volunteer named Esteban sprayed germicide on her scrapes and patched up her numerous skid marks with gauze and tape. He picked bits of gravel out of a couple of the places. She knew she was going to be sore as a boil tomorrow, but right now she focused on the woman to her left.

Sergeant Hanson looked up from the report she was completing on a tablet. She was young enough to have been one of Esbeth's former students. She wore her blond hair back in a severe bun, but her skin was smooth and unblemished, emphasized by her not wearing makeup of any kind. "That's an odd thing to ask. Why do you say that?"

"Let me put it this way. I'm willing to make a side bet with you."

"About what?"

"That before the day is out, either you or I or both of us, will be chatting with a US marshal."

"That's an even more astounding thing to say."

"That's me, astounding Esbeth."

"Say, I recognize the name now. Aren't you the lady who got quite a bit of publicity a while back for solving a couple of cases that had the police and sheriff's department stumped?" She looked down at the form. "Esbeth Walters. Some sort of amateur detective?" She had very bright blue eyes that probably could smile nicely when not so intense.

"I'm just glad you didn't say 'little old lady.' I get that a lot, though I'm neither all that little nor that old."

"Well, I hope you let us handle this one. We're more suited to handle an accident like this."

"That's what I'm trying to get through to you. That this was no accident."

"I think you'd better go home and lie down. This has all been pretty trying for you."

"Thank you very much for the patronization, but I'll add another observation, if you don't mind."

"Go ahead." She no longer tapped at the tablet's screen but stared back with all the patience of Job waiting on a cab.

"I'll bet you would very much like to be a detective sergeant. Perhaps you've even been reading books on forensics and studying for the test."

"That is just a wild... and lucky guess."

"Well, look around here closely, my young dear, because there is a lot you're missing."

E sbeth sat in her power chair with a hot cup of tea beside her as she waited for *Jeopardy!* to come on when the knock came at her door.

"Come in," she yelled.

Of course they didn't. She had to struggle to her feet, as stiff and tender as she'd ever felt at once. "Well, hush my puppies," she muttered to herself.

She swung the door open, and there stood Sergeant Hanson, only she'd changed out of her blue uniform and wore street clothes, jeans, a white blouse, and red cowgirl boots.

"Can I come in?" She'd let her hair down, too, and had added a touch of makeup, just enough to keep the natural look that favored her youthful face. The blond hair swept out in a graceful wave behind her as she came in when Esbeth gave her an inviting wave of her hand.

"Want a cup of tea?"

"No... Well, okay. I'd love one."

She must have read that accepting someone's offer often endeared them to you. Esbeth didn't mind. The pot was still hot, and she thought it impolite to sip alone. Without being asked, she added a dollop of honey as she had to her own cup.

Hanson half rose from the sofa and took the offered cup. Esbeth sat back in her chair, peeking at the clock. Alex Trebek would probably have to wait for another day. This might take a moment or two.

"You've got questions?" Esbeth asked.

Chapter 10: An Elephant in the Room

"I want to know how you knew about the US marshals." She took a polite sip of tea. One eyebrow rose. "This is quite good."

Esbeth held back the comment she almost made, about being all out of hemlock at the moment. She'd get over missing one TV show out of her life. She cleared her throat. "I used to teach math, so it makes me lean to the logical. I had a hypothesis."

"Which was…?"

"Why would a grown man endure such silly makeup to be a not particularly good mime? Why would someone deliberately run off the street and over such a man? Why was the man doing his bad mime bit at that particular location?"

Hanson held her teacup halfway to her mouth, now frozen in midair. "And what did you conclude?"

"Oh, my dear, I wasn't as far as a conclusion yet. Can I ask, did you find so much as a fingerprint or bit of forensic evidence in the car?"

"No. Wiped clean." She caught herself. "I didn't do the investigating myself, but I was curious and peeked at a copy of the report once I was done talking to the federal marshal."

"Here's another ponderable. Why was that particular car used? I would think it would be quickly traceable back to its owner. Probably stolen. So why use it and not some other heap parked anywhere along the streets?"

"I… I don't know. I didn't think that was significant. It was stolen, of course. Report got filed about the same time as the accident… or whatever it was. What do you think?"

"I think it was an elephant in the room. You ask anyone who saw the incident and they will remember the car in detail. It helps that it sat there after the crime. But ask about the driver and I'd guess you get very little."

"Doodly-squat."

"Is that the technical term for it?"

"It'll do." The sergeant put her cup down without taking the sip she'd intended. "Look, first of all, my name's Betty Jo, but you can call me Bette."

"Thanks. That's a step forward."

"Let's go out on a limb here," Bette said. "Can you be frank with me about what you think went on there? I don't care how wild and crazy it seems. I just want to hear your raw and unveiled take on this."

"Well..." Esbeth took a sip of her tea, since it was starting to cool. "My half-baked theory is that the late mime, and forgive me for disliking mimes, was in the witness protection program, waiting to testify against someone. Either the person threatened by the testimony or the person unnamed who he or she hired was driving that vehicle, which is a shame because it looked to be a fine classic car that didn't deserve that treatment."

"Hmmm."

"I'll bet the marshal didn't share the man's real identity with you, did he?"

"No. No, he didn't."

"Here's something else." Esbeth peeked at the clock. No sense turning the TV on now. They'd be waiting for the Final Jeopardy clue. She could hear the music in her head. "If I were a young, ambitious policewoman wanting to make a name for myself, I might pursue one of two avenues. I imagine the borrowed auto is a dead end, as intended. So I might follow up on the squashed mime and see if any identity could be found, though I suspect that is a dead end as well, if you will please forgive the horrible pun."

"And the other way?"

"I would seek a list of names and addresses of all the mothers who were in that park in the play area. The one reason a man like that might go through the shame of being a bad mime is to perhaps catch glimpses of his wife and child, or mistress at the very least. He was probably supposed to keep away from them so they couldn't be used against him to keep him from testifying."

Bette rocked back in her seat an inch. "Oh. Why didn't I think of that? But wouldn't she have gone into the program with him?"

"Not if the child's birth was a secret, one he even kept from the marshals as well as his wife."

E sbeth pushed her cart out of the grocery exit and saw the squad car parked next to her car. One uniformed cop sat on the back end of the vehicle. Another taller male stood way down at the end of the parking lot. A puff of smoke rose from his face and was tugged away by the breeze.

"Let me guess. You checked all the women whose names you had from the park, and none of them admitted being connected to the mime." Esbeth unlocked her car and started loading her cloth bags of groceries into the passenger seat and the floor in front of it.

"If you knew that...?" Sergeant Hanson rose off the police car and stepped closer.

"I didn't then. And there's a chance you talked to the person, though it's a slim chance. You seem a pretty sharp cookie."

"But you don't think I found her, do you?"

"No." Esbeth closed the door and started to push the cart to the holder for empty carts next to her car. No accident. She always parked in the same place when she could. "You don't even have a for-sure identity on who the mime really was, do you?"

"How do you know that?"

"US marshals are about as chatty as FBI agents. Everything's on a need-to-know basis, and you don't need to know. Right?"

Hanson nodded.

"I'll bet you got a stay-away encouragement from your lieutenant as well. Told you to leave it alone, didn't he?" Esbeth managed not to grin at the confirming surprise on Hanson's face.

"You must be quite a clever detective when you get going," Hanson said.

"Oh, I have my days. But truth is, you're kind of like me, which I admire. Someone tells you to butt out, you get your back up and want to know more than ever."

"Why are you that way? I know why I am."

"It's because I don't have children or grandchildren, nothing to dote on in my busybody years. So I just naturally nose around where I'm not supposed to. And this happened right in front of me, almost on top of me."

Hanson glanced to the end of the parking lot. The tall cop there was stepping on a cigarette butt and twisting his toe. "That's McPerry. He smokes. This little stop gave him a chance to indulge." He started to come toward them.

"He's not in on this, is he? This is on your own hook?"

Hanson hesitated then nodded.

"Give me a call and tell me when you have a day off where you can be wearing your civies. Come by and get me, and I'll show you one thing you might try."

"Tomorrow," Hanson muttered in a low voice. She opened the squad car door and started to slide in.

McPerry came up to them. The half-repressed look of disdain on his face told her that Bette had told him about Esbeth. Esbeth the detective. She shrugged it off. Esbeth turned and climbed into her car. She'd bought some fresh basil for a pasta dish, and the whole inside of the car smelled of it.

Chapter 11: Facing a Gun's Barrel

Esbeth got to the park bench early. It gave her time to get that squid-and-seaweed salad she'd missed out on the other day. It also meant fending off grackles while she ate it. They were big, black noisy birds that flew close and landed to strut around her ankles, hoping for her to drop a scrap or two.

"There you are."

Esbeth looked up. This time Bette wore a blue denim shirt and khaki slacks along with her off-duty red boots.

The grackles took off in an irritated flurry as Bette walked up to the bench and sat down beside Esbeth. She held a Starbucks container and took a sip. "What did you think we might find here, back at the scene of the crime?"

"Why did you decide to join the police force?"

Bette lowered the cup, looked hard at Esbeth. "My dad was a cop, but knowing you, I imagine you already know that. The bigger deal is he did so back when the police department motto was 'protect and serve.' You don't hear that too much anymore, but I still buy into it. That's why I wear the uniform, and... that's why I'm here right now. So spill."

"Go ahead and take a gander all about you, see what you can spot."

Bette's eyes narrowed as she swept the park. No one was entertaining in the open theater at the moment, and a couple of young boys were skateboarding through the area, in spite of signs that told them not to do so. Her head stopped moving when she fixed on a young redheaded woman on a bench beside the children's playground. The woman had skin so pale the freckles stood out from quite a distance. Her long straight hair hung and flowed down to the middle of her back. "Her. That woman there! She's been crying, is reaching for her handkerchief right now."

"You think she's sad because of that little black-haired, brown-eyed boy she's been watching play, who seems to be having a ball, the one she's already hugged a couple of times as if he might float away at any second?"

"You're good. I'll give you that." Bette's frank blue eyes fixed on Esbeth from barely a foot away. "Now what?"

"Well, I'd wish you luck, but I suspect and fear you won't have any."

She frowned at Esbeth and rose off the bench, left her coffee behind, and went over to the young woman.

Esbeth watched them talk. The young woman, already emotional, appeared to grow agitated, while Bette looked like she was trying to calm her. The woman called the boy over, clutched him close, then rose and held his hand as they walked off.

Bette came back, looked down at Esbeth. "I guess I should have known. If she didn't come forward the first time, there had to be a reason. I told her I was only trying to help. Do you know what she told me?"

Esbeth shook her head.

"She said her late mother once told her, 'Not every man is trying to stop you because you're a woman, and not every woman is trying to help you because she's on your side.' Can you believe that?"

"As a matter of fact, yes."

"Now I won't know her story or even where she lives."

"You can bet she lives close to here." Esbeth took her empty plastic lunch container over to the trash bin. The grackles followed her. She liked grackles about as much as she liked clowns. One grackle had followed her across a parking lot once, walking right behind her. When she'd stop to look back, it would stop and cock its head at her. This stop-and-start behavior went on for a few more feet, very Alfred Hitchcock, until Esbeth figured it out. The darn thing was listening for her to step on the fallen acorns in the parking lot so it could get at her meat. Still, it had half spooked her out of her socks at first.

T he young woman—well, girl, practically—didn't come back with her son for three days. That didn't bother Esbeth. What else did she have on her dance calendar anyway but to wait around?

Playgrounds drew little boys like giant magnets. Esbeth didn't expect they'd stay away too long. This boy looked about two, going on three, and had his papa's looks, she guessed.

"Marik. Marik," the woman called. The boy came running, held his mother's hand as they started off. Esbeth hung back, finally stood once they were nearly out of sight down the street.

"Gosh, I'm a nosy old biddy," she thought to herself. Half a block later, that changed to "Hush my puppies. I should get out and walk more." Parts of her still ached from her recent roll and tumble. Other parts had stiffened from sitting too long, that and not being in shape. Just getting on in years, at a rate that surprised her, took care of the rest.

Still, what did she hope to gain from this? Well, at bottom, she suspected someone somewhere had left a job half-finished, had maybe not known about the girl at first but had maybe figured it out by now. She wouldn't intrude if everything was okay. On the other hand, she hadn't quite figured out what she would do if it wasn't okay.

"Probably nothing," she said to herself then took it back as the young woman went in the door of a small blue house, closing it after her and little Marik. Across the street, a man got out of a car. He wore black pants and black shoes that went with his black jacket. Who wore a jacket these days in Austin's heat? Only those who maybe wanted to hide a shoulder holster. Esbeth sought to move faster. But she ran like a worn truck these days; there just weren't that many gears after second.

Maybe it was just a marshal, but it didn't look like it, and the car was wrong. It looked like a rental. Plus, the front door to the house had been left open a crack as Esbeth got to it. She paused a moment on the front sidewalk to bend and grab her knees, take deep gulping breaths. She had told herself to never get old, but look what happened. While in her pause, she straightened and lifted the mailbox lid. Inside were bills and junk mail for Gretchen Jones. That gave her the final piece of the puzzle. She headed for the door.

"It's all my fault. I should have never let him say a thing."

Esbeth figured that for Gretchen's voice. She swung the door open and barged into Gretchen's house. "Mail lady," she called out.

Chapter 12: You're No Mail Lady

The figure in black turned. Esbeth had been right about one thing, wrong about another. It wasn't a man. A woman stood there in the black suit, but she held a gun and didn't look anything like a US marshal. She did look full of trouble and danger, though.

The woman spun and pointed the gun at Esbeth. "You're no mail lady. Get over there." She swung the gun to point toward where Gretchen and the small boy stood. The boy squirmed to get loose, but his mother held him tight.

Esbeth complied. At one earlier moment, in all the things her head was trying to do at once, she had considered that maybe the chances of Gretchen getting shot would go down with Esbeth being present. But when she took a look at the face of the woman holding the gun, she began to doubt that.

"You're Mrs. Luiz, aren't you?" Esbeth asked.

"Carmita," Gretchen said, her voice shaky and low.

"How d'you know thah?" Just a trace of an accent in Carmita's voice. Her long black hair was tucked inside the back of her black suit jacket. She stared at Esbeth.

If Esbeth had seen her closer up earlier and with better eyes than she had these days she might have had a better handle on everything before now. But it was all clearer now, and the tiny shake in Carmita's hand that held the gun didn't encourage Esbeth; it had the opposite effect.

"Who are you?" Gretchen asked Esbeth.

"Just someone who thought you might need help right now. I wasn't wrong, as it turns out. Wish I could be more encouraging, though. Ramón's the boy's father, right?"

"Ramón is also my husband. *Mi esposo*," Carmita snarled. "Who is dead now because of this one."

"How can you say that when you're the one who ran him down?" Esbeth wished she had said nothing as soon as she closed her mouth.

"Shut up. Shut up. *Basta*." Carmita's face flushed a bright pink. She lifted the gun, fired a shot straight up. *Bam!* Dust and bits of plaster sprinkled down from the hole in the ceiling. She lowered the gun, yet its menace remained.

Esbeth glanced toward the mother and son. Marik had quit struggling now, and his eyes grew wide, and his mouth puckered and quivered, ready to cry.

"They sent us to Portland. In that witless protection program." She probably meant to say it that way. "It's in Oregon. Did you know it rains a lot there? But could Ramón stay there? No. He runs back to this one. And now..."

Carmita raised the gun she held and pointed it their way. Though it shook, Esbeth closed her eyes, couldn't help herself. As a result, she missed seeing what happened in the scuffling noise she heard at the other end of the room. She opened her eyes. There stood Bette Hanson and her partner McPerry wrestling Carmita to the carpet, where the gun already lay.

Esbeth breathed in and realized she had stopped breathing way too long ago.

"Thanks a bunch, Bette," Esbeth managed. "I thought I'd really stepped in the deep water this time."

"You had. But you were lucky. I'd asked McPerry to swing by the park every now and then. We saw you take off up the street like a turtle on fire, the woman there ahead of you."

"Let me introduce Gretchen Jones and her son, Marik." Esbeth swept a hand toward the young redheaded woman.

Carmita growled and tried to bite McPerry's hand as he stood her upright. He snapped the hand back in time.

"You want to catch me up on a few of the many details I'm going to have to have a handle on before I talk to my lieutenant and no doubt some ticked-off US marshals?"

"Ramón was your CPA. Right?" Esbeth asked Gretchen.

She nodded. Tears ran down both freckled cheeks. She held on tight to Marik, who continued to squirm.

"You started a day care center when Marik was born, then got an offer to buy it, one you couldn't believe, couldn't refuse. Right?"

Gretchen nodded. "Twice what it was worth. I had to sell."

"But Ramón thought something was fishy. He wanted to go to the authorities. You finally agreed."

Gretchen was shaking so hard she couldn't speak now, but she nodded.

"You'd better cut to the chase, Esbeth. Backup is on the way." Bette nodded toward the door. Esbeth could hear a siren approaching outside.

"There's a big stink in Mexico about day-care centers allegedly being sites for money laundering by drug cartels like the Sinaloa Cartel that shuffles tons of drugs up into the US. The US Treasury Department can put places like that on a blacklist, as they did. In my reading, I had come across rumors that something similar might be tried here, and suddenly a whole lot of day-care centers were being bought up, often with huge cash payments. I've been following this in the media. It used to be nightclubs and other venues where lots of money flowed through when money got laundered. But someone came up with this clever plan. The wrinkle here was that Ramón had too much integrity for that. He reported the sale, and I'm guessing he was going to have to testify."

"Do you read everything in the news that might relate to crime?" Bette said.

"Don't you?" Esbeth said.

"Integrity," Carmita spat. "He had me and two *real* children of his own. We ended up in Portland."

"It's a nice city, I've heard," McPerry said, not helping matters at all.

"But Ramón wouldn't stay up there," Esbeth said. "He missed Gretchen and Marik here. Must have driven all the way down to see them. I'm guessing Carmita flew, and probably, for that little necessary touch of irony, left her kids in a day care center up there. The distracting car she picked to steal for the hit and the clothes she wore hinted at premeditated. She had me thinking I'd seen a button man for a cartel there for a spell. That kept all this from being handled by local police, as it should have been. I'm guessing she even has a return ticket to Portland."

Carmita switched to Spanish. Though Esbeth knew some of the words, she sure hoped little Marik didn't.

Two more cops in uniform came in the door, weapons drawn. Once they got the nod from Bette, they put their weapons away and helped McPerry take Carmita out to a cruiser.

"Well, I guess you did some good here after all," Bette said.

Esbeth looked at Gretchen, who had dropped to her knees and clutched Marik. She cried and shook hard as she clutched the boy, who had given up on squirming and hugged her back. "I like to think so," Esbeth said, "but I'm never really sure."

Chapter 13: This Spud's for You

The body still lay out in the center of the bridge when Esbeth pulled her car over to the side of the road in the middle of a string of sheriff's department vehicles. It was the body of a well-nourished man wearing a burgundy shirt and blue jeans. His big oval silver belt buckle was catching a lot of direct sunlight and throwing sparkles. She could see that much from where she got out of her car. The bridge was a hundred feet long, the body at the halfway point. Just a couple of men in uniform crouched near the body. Esbeth's sight was still good that way, though she couldn't brag as much about her hearing. She looked up into the sky, light blue and cloudless. An oversized sun beat down on them, hot and relentless. At least no buzzards were circling. Yet.

"What's she doing here?" Sheriff Danvers shouted all the way to her as he stood up from beside the late Boyd Wembly. He cast a pretty firm shadow himself, could well have been nosing up to the same trough as Boyd. "Someone get her out of here," he yelled to his chief deputy, Bob Clanton, who stood beside Danvers. Maybe it was rhetorical, because Bob made no move toward her. Neither did any of the others in the area.

Esbeth looked out across the desert patch of country around them. She could see figures moving about in the distance among the mesquite and sage, some down in the flat dry river bed. Yellow soil and loose sandy rocks and cacti dotted the open stretches between what passed for trees.

"I guess out here it's more unusual to find a river *with* water in it than without," Alex said. She slammed the passenger door. Esbeth had brought her along because she wanted to see Esbeth in action, as she had put it. Her short-cropped hair gave her a boyish, sprightly charm. She was trim, young, and athletic—probably not a contrast Esbeth needed to encourage around herself. But she had proven herself a bedrock friend so far, which went the longest possible way with Esbeth.

When Esbeth swung back to Danvers, he was stomping her way, still yelling for Bob or anyone to *do something*. He was glaring not at Esbeth but over at where Scott was taking his pictures for the newspaper. "Did you call her? Hey, Scotto. Yeah, I'm talking to you." He was almost up to them, his voice booming. Alex took a half step back.

On the way out, Esbeth had told her about the sheriff, told her that some folks thought that if brains were leather, he wouldn't have enough to saddle a flea. But she didn't repeat any of that now.

"Oh, don't get all whomper jawed," Esbeth said. "Did you forget already that I helped you on a case or two before, let you get all the credit?"

Did you ever see a fellow pinch a finger in a cabinet or something, know it was his own fault, and not be able to say anything? That was the look on Danvers's face. Once he'd taken a deep breath, he said, "Any blind pig can find the acorn once in a while."

"To think that the mighty oak was once a nut like me," Esbeth said, trying to act like the seventy-year-old lady she was.

That made him squint. But the worst for him was that his debt was too big. He *did* owe her, and that stung him to the quick.

"Don't try to be ironic," he finally managed, a little slow on the comeback. He looked like he wanted to go into great detail about why, but a couple of deputies were bringing over a tall lean fellow in a worn denim shirt. Like any recent crime scene, activity was abuzz all around them.

"When I come back, we can discuss this," Sheriff Danvers said. He pushed past them and took off in a brisk, ticked-off walk.

At least he had not given her the boot from the area, no matter that he had the right and was tempted. But he did kind of owe her. While he was occupied, she made steps toward the victim, Alex tagging along. "Does he know what 'ironic' means?" she said. "Folks may be right. Unless that's a clever cover-up, it looks like someone liposuctioned the brain out of that one."

Just as they were about to step onto the bridge itself, one of those with stone walls running along each side as guard rails, Alex pointed to one of those Don't Mess with Texas anti-littering signs. Below it lay a can of hair spray and a crumpled sack. "Now, there's irony for you," Alex said.

"I'd be careful about jumping to any conclusions about Danvers," Esbeth cautioned. "I might have made a mistake saying what I did about him. I don't want you to think for a moment that he's some sort of cartoon character or anything. He can be just as dangerous as any man, more than most in fact."

Up close, once they were near the body, it looked like the victim had wrapped himself around a six-pack more than once. The pearl buttons of his shirt were stretched across some substantial acreage of burgundy shirt. The deputy beside the body started to say something, gave a sigh instead.

"Alex, meet Deputy Bob Clanton," Esbeth said.

He flicked his eyes over Alex, registering the way her short dark hair was being tousled by the wind, the way her athletic build filled her slacks and blouse. "Pleased," he said to Alex.

To Esbeth, he said, "Morning, Miss Walters. Whatever in the world brings you all the way out this way?"

"Nice ostrich-hide cowboy boots," Alex noted. She was staring down at the large speed bump Boyd Wembly had become. Esbeth focused on one of the clenched hands of the corpse and thought she saw a tiny corner of white paper between the thumb and forefinger.

Esbeth looked up at the sound of steps. Scott was moving closer, was careful to step around a stone bigger than an egg laying near the body.

"What killed him?"

Scott nodded down toward the loose stone. "Murder weapon, they think," he mumbled.

"Don't touch or move anything. You both probably shouldn't be this close."

"How many sticks of gum have you got in your mouth?" Esbeth asked.

He didn't answer, looked away as if a photo shot might be developing. Then she noticed the copter sweeping down, kicking up dust, passing over in a throbbing, whirring roar she could hear now. It swept on along the dry river, kicking up a fair amount of dust, until it was out of sight.

"Not coming for the body?" Alex asked. The sun was highlighting the smooth skin of her face. Esbeth caught Scott giving her a glance, knew darned well why he wasn't smoking, now also knew why he'd called her to butt in on a case where she wasn't welcome.

"No," Esbeth explained. "The ME hasn't even been here yet. They're probably sweeping with FLIR. That's 'forward-looking infrared radar.' If anyone's hiding out there around us, they'll be able to mark the body heat, pin down a location."

Esbeth moved over to the stone guardrail, saw a small black square of rolled tape near the bottom edge. She stepped closer, peered out over the side of the bridge. It wasn't that far of a drop to the riverbed below, though she doubted if she could reach up this high herself if standing down there. She pushed herself up over the concrete abutment. It was only waist high, but her one-time pear shape had since become more pumpkin, so it was all she could do to hang over a ways and peer down below her.

"With all this gear and technology these days, they ought to be able to figure this out in minutes," Alex said, shaking her head.

"Young lady"—the voice belonged to Danvers, who had hiked back to them—"whoever you are to be drug out here into the middle of this.

Solving any case can take days, sometimes weeks, no matter what Miss Walters has been filling your head with. Now you're all going to have to move back off this bridge 'til the ME gets here. You too, Scott."

They all moved off the bridge as ordered, which brought them closer to where Bob Clanton was talking with the lean man.

"What do you think happened, Ben?" Esbeth heard Bob ask.

"I didn't think nothin' at first. I was up on the hill thar"—the lean fellow pointed at a spot half a mile up on a ridge—"had been patchin' the barbed wire all along that fence line all mornin'. I looked up and saw Boyd fly backward and land just the way you see him. Time I got down here, he hadn't moved, wasn't gonna. I went to the house, rang for you guys."

"But how do you think it happened?" Bob pressed.

"Dang if I know. Slingshot maybe? I don't know. Like I said, I didn't see it happen."

Esbeth looked back to the body, the stone beside it. Boyd was a big man, but he was no Goliath. She wondered, though, if somewhere he didn't have his David.

Chapter 14: Is That a Snake's Tail?

Sheriff Danvers moved closer to the group of them, looked like he had a question or two. But his head swung back to the road at the sound of the squeal of tires coming toward them. A classic red Ford pickup, late fifties but in mint shape, was barreling their way. Then it veered toward the right, slewed a bit as its tires hit gravel. It skidded in the gravel, swung to its side, and kept sliding and throwing gravel until the back bed corner of the trunk scrunched into the tail lights of one of the patrol cars. The driver's door flew open, and a woman hopped out. She started running for them.

"Just what…" Danvers's mouth hung slightly open.

"That was your cruiser, wasn't it?" Scott said.

That snapped Danvers out of his trance. He started in a brisk way toward the advancing woman. Deputy Clanton dropped what he was doing and moved to help intercept the woman.

"Mrs. Wembly," Scott said to Esbeth softly. "Lucy."

Esbeth was looking over the lean man. He was skinny enough to have to stand twice to cast a shadow.

Scott opened the small, folded paper in his pocket, looked at something he'd scribbled there. "That's Ben Sharpe," he added in a whispered footnote.

Ben looked poured into his jeans. The sleeves of his shirt were short on him as well. Esbeth eased closer to the man. He was staring down the road to where Danvers and Clanton had their hands full holding back the woman who had jumped out the open door of the truck.

"Nice threads," Esbeth said to Ben.

"Humpf." His head snapped back to Esbeth. Then he looked down at himself. "You tryin' to be a funny person?"

"I don't just try," Esbeth said. "I *am* a funny person."

Maybe that wouldn't have flown if she didn't probably look like a white-haired fire plug from where he stood towering over her. As it was, a grin cracked in the tanned road map of wrinkles that was his face. He looked to be in his forties, the kind of fellow who had been dropped on his head by life a few times, the kind who once long ago would have been a saddle-bum cowhand, living on beans all week and whiskey on the weekends. Esbeth liked the look of him right away. He was as much a part of the Southwest as the sandy yellow dirt and scattered cacti. Without knowing any more about him than she did, she had him figured for an angel or a devil, maybe both on given days. He wore a beaten ball cap that proclaimed, "I'd Rather Push a Ford Than Drive a Chevy," which didn't mark him as one of life's deep intellectuals. But then, she hadn't expected a field hand to be spouting square roots.

"These ol' thangs are only fer workin'," he said. "Got 'em from some stuff was layin' 'round, left by... the hand was 'round here before."

"You work for the Wemblys?"

"Sure enough do, ma'am."

"For long?"

"Nope." He was answering kindly enough but not volunteering anything.

"How long?"

"'Bout a week or two."

Now imagine that. Being unable to tell the difference about something like that, and Esbeth had no reason to disbelieve him in this case. His clear pale blue eyes that stood out so in the dark tan of his face, didn't seem to have a lie in them, even though they flicked away from her a couple of times to check on the brouhaha down the road with Mrs. Wembly.

Esbeth could hear her screams of denial from where she stood. "He can't be dead. Can't. Can't. Can't."

When Esbeth looked back from where Danvers and Clanton were still tangled up with Mrs. Wembly, she caught Ben giving Alex a healthy stare. Scott lowered his camera and eased over closer.

"How long was he the hand?" Esbeth said, seeking to get Ben back on track before he got to itching for something he wasn't willing to scratch for.

"Who?"

"The hired hand before you."

"Oh. Quite a while."

"Lucy!" Esbeth heard Deputy Bob yell.

Mrs. Wembly must have given them one of those fake left, dodge right moves. She shot by Esbeth, going like a house afire. Not that Esbeth could have stopped her if she'd wanted to.

Esbeth could hear Danvers popping a gasket behind them, yelling for some of the troops to drop what they were doing and help.

Bob trotted past, and Danvers came puffing along behind. The widow was sprawled across her late husband. Having been through these road shows before, Esbeth thought it would be a good idea to give the law a little room to operate. They could get a little space sensitive when not everything was going hunky-dory. And it rarely did in a murder investigation.

Esbeth gave Alex a nod and eased toward the edge of the bridge. Scott eased along with them. Esbeth already knew why he wasn't carrying his usual pack of Chesterfields. Esbeth had dropped in at Alex's bookstore/coffee shop a few times since meeting her. On a couple of occasions, she'd found Scott there. "Just having a cup," he'd said, a bit defensively. Right. No reason a weathered journalist like him shouldn't hang out at a feminist bookstore.

"Where to now?" Alex asked.

Esbeth had her head down, was following the edge of the bridge. When she stopped abruptly, both Alex and Scott about ran into her.

"What's that? A snake trail?" Alex was looking down to what Esbeth had spotted, a weaving row of dots, mostly swept away, though a stretch a foot long still showed here and there in what dust the passing copter hadn't messed up.

"Yeah," Esbeth said, "kind of."

Esbeth picked her way through the loose rocks, glad to have on her Red Wing boots, just the thing for this terrain.

"Watch for rattlers," she cautioned.

From above them, they could hear shouts from Lucy between the gusts of wind that swept away some of her words.

Out of nowhere, Alex asked, "Do you think people ever have normal lives together, as husband and wife? I mean, look at the divorce rate, at some of the strange situations you run into."

If Esbeth hadn't been staring down at the ground still, she might have shared a pensive look. She could hear how quiet Scott was being, though he followed closely. "That's not fair for me to address," Esbeth said. "I have no personal experience base. But I can tell you, as an outsider, that the concept has its attractions. But I gather it's a lot more work to make it happen right than most people are ready for."

It felt calm and peaceful for a while down along the base of the bridge. Esbeth could see where the floods had smoothed the rocks a bit but not as much as if the river flowed all the time. Where mud stretches had formed, the soil was stretched and dried into flat cracked chunks like sunbaked skin. From where they were, they could look up at the bridge.

"From down here, it's not such a tall bridge, is it?" Alex said. "Why have a bridge at all?"

"Scott," Esbeth said.

"It's a wash," he supplied. "First time we have one of those cow-pissing-on-a-flat-rock rains," he said, showing off for Alex just a bit, Esbeth thought, "and the ground all around here's hard as a congressman's heart. You'll have flood waters running through here you wouldn't believe." He pointed up at the row of holes that ran at intervals all along the bridge. "That's what those are for, drainage during those floods, and to keep the bridge from being stressed by the sudden flow if the water rises enough to press against it or sweep over the bridge. It can be like a little tidal wave down here."

"Alex," Esbeth said. "You're about the right size. Can you reach up that high?"

"As what?"

"As to the top of the bridge?"

"Not quite."

"You Scott?"

"Maybe, if I..."

"Stood on something," Alex finished. She saw Esbeth looking around for the marks where any big rocks might have been moved. "You think someone climbed up there from here and conked him on the head with that little rock?"

"What I'm thinking about," Esbeth said, "is what he was doing out here in the middle of nowhere in the first place."

"Well, what're we looking for," she said.

"Something we already found," Esbeth said. "Be careful where you step." She turned and started back.

The kind of woman Alex was, she followed Esbeth out of the riverbed, stepping in her footsteps without asking her why. Scott came right behind.

As they climbed back up to the road, Danvers and Clanton were leading Lucy along, having gotten her away from her husband. Esbeth could see the medical examiner's Cherokee pull up behind the row of cruisers. Lucy was looking at Esbeth, probably wondering what a little old lady was doing being allowed to tromp around in a crime scene area.

Danvers was probably wondering the same thing, sorry he'd ever let her help him out of a hole before.

"Some questions for you," Danvers was finishing as he led her along.

"I have one for you now," Esbeth said to Lucy, interrupting the sheriff. He was as happy about that as you'd expect.

Lucy still seemed to be a bit in shock. Her glazed eyes swung to Esbeth, but Lucy was ready to respond.

"What can you tell me about the Krugerrands?" Esbeth said.

Chapter 15: About the Gold

Boy, it was like Esbeth had sloshed Lucy across the face with a cold wet washcloth. Clanton and Danvers were fixed on Esbeth and had to unglue to realize Lucy was trying to pull away.

Her head tossed right and left as she thrashed. They got her calmed down and held her still. To Danvers, Lucy said, "Do I have to answer to her?"

"You might as well," he said, "and get it over with." But he was interested, real interested.

Once Lucy had settled down, she stared right at Esbeth, daring her, kind of. "We had a hand, Luke," she said. "Luke Spiven, who'd been with us for a longish spell. He thought... He wanted us to help him with going to college. We... Boyd said no. He left, kind of abrupt like. Boyd said he'd made off with some coins he collected."

"Boyd had Krugerrands?" Danvers said. "How many?"

"Oh, I don't rightly know. Sixty or so. Maybe more."

"How wide of a net have you cast around here?" Esbeth butted in to ask Danvers. "Have you checked every..."

The look that shot across Lucy's face was worth seeing. She spun to Danvers. "Okay," she said. "I done it. We'd been fighting all week. It came to this. I hit him with a tire iron. Or a hammer. I disremember which. I'll tell you what you need to know."

"Bob here is going to take you over to the car there, the one you wrinkled up a bit with your truck, and take a statement. Aren't you, Bob."

The deputy led her away. That left them all standing there with the bewildered-looking Ben Sharpe.

"I *was* wondering why it took her so long between the time of Ben telling her Boyd was dead to her getting here," Esbeth said.

"Think she was getting rid of the real murder weapon?" Danvers believed that as much as Esbeth did.

"No," Esbeth snapped.

He was frowning down at the road then looked up at Esbeth. "Where'd you come up with that business about Krugerrands?" he said.

"If you want a sample," Esbeth said, "check the watch pocket of Mr. Sharpe here."

Danvers's large head swung slowly to the hand, stared at him. Ben squinted, tried to glare back, then let it go. His bony muscled hand slid down and eased out the coin, held it out to the sheriff. The Krugerrand lay there in his palm, glistened in golden sparkles in the glare of the sun. It was one of the big pre-1980 one-ounce coins.

Esbeth doubted if any magician who ever yanked a kicking rabbit out of a top hat got a better effect out of it than she did from those in the small circle of them.

"Great gobs of galloping horned toads," Danvers said. "I knew Boyd was tighter than Fat Foggle's Stetson band but didn't know he was squirreling Rands." To Ben, he snapped, "Where'd you come by that?"

Ben said nothing. His squint had become a glare again, which he was sharing with Esbeth at the moment.

Esbeth gave him a moment to speak for himself. When he didn't take it, she said, "When he came down here to see what was up with Boyd, it was lying over there at the edge of the rail, stuck to the ground with a piece of tape. If you look real close, you can still see the imprint of a springbok from the verso side of the coin on the tape."

"Verso?" Danvers said.

"The tail or reverse side," Scott supplied.

"With pants that tight, it wasn't hard to spot a coin that size tucked away in the watch pocket," Esbeth said, "once I knew one had probably been here."

"What *was* it doing here?" Danvers asked.

"Ben here didn't put it here, did you?" Esbeth said.

"No, ma'am." He looked a little relieved, used probably to being the one to whom the finger usually pointed.

"All morning seems like a long time to be patching up just that little stretch of fence up there," Esbeth said.

"Some folks is quicker'n others, I 'spect. I'm no rocket."

"When you were up there on that hill and looked down to see Ben flying backward, did you hear any sound?" Esbeth asked.

"No," he said then thought about it. "But I guess you could be right. Somethin' must've made me look up."

Danvers held up a hand and then waved for Esbeth to walk a bit off to one side with him. He didn't wave Alex away when she tagged along. "Where are you going with this?" he snapped at Esbeth once they were out of Ben's hearing.

"Same place you are."

"You think you know who the killer was, how it was done? How could you?" He wasn't mad any longer, just puzzled. He'd seen the same things Esbeth had. His eyes flicked from Esbeth to Alex, back to Esbeth.

Esbeth knew she was on dangerous ground, gave it a moment of thought before she said anything. "You weren't a schoolteacher for forty years, that's all. But I'll tell you a couple of things. If you want some good clear prints of your killer, you might dust that can of Aqua Net hairspray that's lying back there beside the road."

He looked back that way then at Esbeth again, shook his head. "I'm not on the same page," he admitted.

"And if you want to find the killer himself," Esbeth said, "you could turn Mrs. Wembly loose, give her some slack rope, but follow her closely. She ought to take you right to him."

Alex was staring at Esbeth like she'd just walked across a pond without getting wet. She was just as amazed at the humble and polite way Danvers was suddenly acting as at what Esbeth had said.

It even took Esbeth a second or two to realize that the scrunched look on Danvers's doughy face was him trying to work up a friendly smile, quite a feat on as salty a buzzard as he could be. "But it ain't Ben."

"No," Esbeth said.

"Well"—and Esbeth could tell this was a crawl on broken glass for him to ask—"what did kill Boyd?"

Esbeth looked back to where the ME and his assistant were crouched over Boyd. In as soft a voice as she could manage, she told Danvers, "A potato gun."

A lex and Esbeth sat on Esbeth's porch watching traffic and the one or two pedestrians willing to brave the heat that could already be felt in spite of it still being early in the a.m.

Esbeth lived far enough out near the edge of Austin to be in the sheriff's turf when anyone's cat got up a tree. Houses were a bit farther apart, which was fine with her, and they didn't get much foot traffic—not all that much auto traffic either.

When she heard a car crunch into the gravel of her driveway, she glanced at Alex.

"Scott," she said.

He came bounding around to the front of the house acting as spry and coltish as Esbeth recalled ever seeing him. For all the years she'd known him, though he was half her age, he usually dragged himself around like he had one log hanging off the truck.

When he had trotted up the stairs, he plopped onto the swing by Alex. Esbeth sat in a wicker chair with cushions outside the front of the picture window. It was the kind of chair that when you got into it at her age, you had better plan to stay a while. It had been a gift from someone. She didn't really care for it much, but she was never going to wear it out unless she sat in it.

Scott dropped a folded newspaper onto the seat between them. Alex snatched at it. Esbeth knew the ink wouldn't be wet, but it might be still warm. It was early enough that the morning paper would barely be on some newsstands. Usually, Scott procrastinated when forced to write a story. Photography was his real line. But he had scrambled in an abnormal flurry late yesterday in order to get this story ready for page one.

"They catch him yet?" Alex asked. She was in her early thirties. Either the shadowed light on the porch or sitting next to Scott was making her look ten years younger.

Scott laughed. "Danvers and his men are shooting all around the county like so many greased bars of soap. But they're no closer to catching Luke Spiven than I am to..."

"Growing a full head of hair," Esbeth finished for him.

His mouth snapped shut, and he gave her a look. But the porch was a quieter place for a while. There was only the rustle of Alex poring over the newspaper and an occasional car rolling by.

Chapter 16: The Wrap on a Case

"Listen to this," Esbeth said. "It sounds like the sheriff was right there when it happened. After he tells about following Lucy to the motel and finding where Luke Spiven had been staying, he gives the whole thing. Boyd being lured out there by a note from the kid—the kid was only eighteen—and Boyd going there to find one of his missing Krugerrands taped to a spot that positioned Boyd just right to one of those drainage holes we saw. The stone that killed him was projected through the hole by a 'potato gun' shoved into the hole from the outside of the bridge. The kid worked the switch on the thing with a remote control from behind some mesquite up on the dry river's bank. He then proceeded—that has to be a cop word—to ride a bicycle down to the bridge, grab the murder weapon and note—probably spotted Ben coming, knew there was not enough time to scoop up the bait Rand as well—and biked all the way back to the motel."

She looked up from the paper to Esbeth. "It's just like you told him then. But how did you know that? And you never did tell what a potato gun is, or how you knew that was what had to have been used."

Esbeth nodded to Scott.

"We couldn't put that in the story," he said, "don't want every kid who doesn't know how to make one rushing out to get started with his own. But a lot of kids already know. You take some PVC, that white plastic pipe plumbers use. You need a longish piece of two-inch pipe and a shorter four-inch piece for the chamber. You join them with a reducer neck. On the side of the four-inch chamber section, you install a flint switch, the kind you get in Coleman lanterns. That way a spark will be thrown into the chamber when you've sealed off the back of the chamber, either with a clasping gate or a screw-on cover."

He looked at Alex, saw she was following along closely. "You can mount a silencer to the barrel end if you want. Luke's potato gun probably had one. That'll muffle the noise a bit, but there's still a pop. To fire the thing, you just unscrew the chamber, spray in some hair spray. Aqua Net is a good brand, since it's loaded with butane and isopropane. Then you screw on the chamber lid, flip the firing switch to throw a spark. You get a controlled explosion that fires the potato. Usually, you've rammed a potato all the way down the barrel with a broom handle or something. But you could use a smooth round rock if you packed it in with something to seal the tube."

Alex was still staring at Esbeth. "Well, you sure let the sheriff have his cojones." She shook her head. "But how did you know?"

"People think differently," Esbeth said. "Danvers is a linear thinker, has had years of criminal investigation. He looks for logical answers along the lines of what he has seen, experienced. His tool kit wasn't ready to think about a kid being behind the murder. But when I saw the way Boyd had been lured out to the spot, the artifice of someone taping a coin in just the right place, it didn't speak to me as the actions of a mature mind. That led me to spotting some of the bicycle tracks, even though most of those on the bridge had been wiped carefully away. I also was looking at the drainage hole for marks of something like a potato gun being shoved in place there. It was the only reason I could think of why anyone would want to position a person on that exact spot. It's the kind of cowardly at-a-distance murder a kid might think of, one who is afraid to face his victim. As a longtime schoolteacher, I knew about potato guns, though this is the first one I ever heard of figuring in a murder."

"And the last, I hope," Scott said.

"Were Lucy and the boy lovers or something?" Alex asked.

Scott said, "It's all there in the story."

Alex's head bent, and her eyes swept through the rest of the newspaper account. "The sheriff says"—and she let those words rankle—"that Luke was actually Lucy's son, that she'd had him before she and Boyd were married."

"One of those cactus patch kids," Scott offered, "the kind a woman won't talk about." He let the words trail off when he caught the look he was getting from Alex.

"Apparently," Alex continued, "Lucy had managed to get Luke hired as a hand. Boyd had worked him hard. But at some point, Lucy must have softened and told Luke he was her son. Luke had pushed to get them to send him to college, something he couldn't afford. He'd played on her guilt. But Boyd was too much of a miser to go along with that. So the kid had stolen Boyd's pile of Krugerrands. He'd only been able to afford technical school, had been going there for about half a year before his resentment got the best of him, and he'd sent Boyd a note giving him a time and place, telling him he wanted to give back the Rands. Just listen to Sheriff Danvers taking credit for all this."

"He does have a memory like a frog's tail," Scott said.

"Men," Alex said. She snapped the newspaper shut, shoved it across the table toward Scott.

"What?" he said.

"The sheriff's got a job to do, Alex," Esbeth said. "I don't mind giving him that."

"All you gave Esbeth in the story," she snapped at Scott, "was a tiny line saying she was there and that she'd been instrumental."

"Well, Alex," Scott said, "do you think..."

"Lands, Scott," Esbeth interrupted. "Do you think that was even such a good idea?"

He looked back and forth between Alex and Esbeth, feeling he might be in a no-win scenario, which he was. Then another idea dawned on him slowly, and his widened eyes swung to Esbeth. "You think I might have staked you as a goat?" he said.

Alex ignored him, interrupted him, saying, "I'd just once like to see a man live up to the Wild West heroics they keep billing themselves for instead of riding on someone like Esbeth's coattails."

Scott's forehead bunched. He looked like he might be working on a diplomatic answer. But he stopped himself, stared at a car moving down the street slowly, the driver looking at the numbers on the houses.

Scott grabbed Alex, threw her off the swing onto the cement floor of the porch.

"Scott. You're cruising for a bruising." Alex started to get up, and he pushed her flat again with one hand while he rushed across the porch and knocked Esbeth sideways onto the porch, wicker chair and all. Her sentiments ran along the line Alex had partially expressed. Then she heard a boom like a tire blowing out. The picture window above Esbeth shattered in an explosion, and glass showered across the porch, though much of it fell inside the house.

Tires squealed as the car peeled out.

Esbeth peeked out from the chair she realized was broken in a couple of places, its cushions hanging loose and all over her. The porch floor was full of glass window diamonds. She saw Scott leap clear over the rail to no doubt land right in the middle of a bed of lobelia and dusty miller Esbeth had been all last weekend planting.

She heard Scott's car start and tear out of her driveway in a fish-tailing flurry of gravel. Seconds later, there was a screech and a huge smash of rending metal down the street.

Alex and Esbeth, both on their hands and knees, being careful where they moved because of all the glass, looked at each other then up at the hole that had once been Esbeth's picture window behind where she'd been sitting.

Alex got to her feet and gave Esbeth a tug to get her upright. They got to the porch steps in time to see a thin young man—a boy, really—spring out of the cruising car that was now smashed against a Volvo that had the misfortune of trying to exercise its right-of-way on the street that crossed Esbeth's. Scott's car was pulled up close at an angle behind the collided vehicles.

They were in time to see Scott climb out of his car and take off after the running boy on foot. They were headed in Esbeth's direction. They got to see Scott take a diving leap and tackle the runner.

They wrestled around in the middle of the street. The boy seemed frantic, but Scott had him on size and strength. He was soon holding him down while signaling to the gaping driver of an approaching car to wait a moment.

"Do you think one of you spectators could call Danvers for me?" Scott yelled over to them. "Tell him I've found Luke Spiven for him and that the weapon that killed Boyd Wembly is probably in the car."

Esbeth went inside to make the call. When she came back out, Scott and Alex were escorting Luke up onto the porch. Both of them had a firm grip on him from either side. Esbeth carried a broom and dustpan and started to sweep a clear path. But she managed a glance or two at the boy. She'd like to say his face held some hurt puppy or deer-in-the-headlights look. But his lean hard face, surrounded by bushy dark and unruly hair, only looked mean and intense—a bit of Charles Manson's stare and the insolent glare of a youth who thought the world owed him something. His shirt was torn, and a trickle of blood ran down from one eyebrow. He seemed not to notice. This was a boy, true to form with the way he had murdered Boyd from a distance, who had tried a drive-by shooting with a potato gun.

In the distance, Esbeth could hear the beginning of an approaching siren.

Scott's clothes were as tattered now as Luke's. What hair Scott had stood out in three to four directions. He was looking at Alex. Her earlier feistiness was gone.

"Next time," Scott said to her, and Esbeth thought he did a reasonable job of throttling some of his exasperation, "be more careful what you wish for. You might just get it."

Chapter 17: Should Have Stood in Bed

Esbeth knocked on the door. It swung open to her tapping then stopped against something inside. The breeze on the porch swirled a brown pile of oak leaves in the corner of the porch. The leaves made restless scratching sounds as they scurried and whirled over the worn floorboards. The house was run down, not the way she would have thought Lonnigan Saunders would let any house of his get.

"Lonnie," she called out, pushed at the door, and felt something move against the door inside. A car went by on the street back of her, a long way from where she stood feeling very alone. The porch was in the shadows of the trees that crowded the house, trees that filled the long walk that twisted through the bushes and thick trunks. A chill shook her in spite of the thick sweater she wore, one she'd knitted in the long nights against just such an autumn day as this. Fading sunlight flickered in spots, moving restless and nervous up to the edge of the porch where heavier shadows covered everything, including the wooden rocker that creaked in uneasy motion all by itself. She pushed harder against the door until it suddenly gave way. An arm dropped out of the opening, a bit of brown cloth clenched in the gnarled fist. Esbeth snapped upright then forced herself to stoop closer and stare to make certain that what she was seeing for the first time in almost twenty years was Lon.

She slid her head inside the gaping doorway, too scared to be cautious. He lay stretched across a throw rug and the hardwood floor, his face turned toward her, eyes open, staring but unseeing. His mouth was open, and his face twisted in fear that must have matched her own. His full head of white hair was tousled, stiff strands sticking out in half a dozen directions. It was Lon. The wooden handle of a kitchen knife stuck out of the side of his robe. His hand grasped at it, was frozen there, though it was hard to tell whether he had been trying to pull it out or hold it in place. Esbeth realized she was shaking, taking deep gulping breaths. She backed out of the doorway, turned, and walked as fast as she could, weaving along his walkway toward the street, thinking of the small mom-and-pop store, J & B's Market, she had seen on the corner where she could hope to find a phone somewhere other than at what was soon to be a taped-off crime scene.

Have you ever had one of those days, she was thinking, *well, when you feel you should have just stood in bed?* That was an old-timey way of putting it, but she was kind of an old-timey gal herself. She got to her car, stood beside it for a moment, glad for its familiar outline. Then she started toward the store as fast as she could walk, which, given that today was her 73rd birthday, was no threat to the sound barrier.

Sure, it was her birthday. But her thoughts were not on cakes or on party favors. The sky above looked ominous, the sun entirely gone. Grey bunched clouds covered the sky and were twisted in a mean gnarled scowl, threatening some kind of foul weather.

Lon had thought he was going to marry her once. Well, twice, actually, a long story.

"Do you have a phone?" Esbeth said, rushing through the store's door, jangling a row of bells they kept on the door. A roundish fellow in his late fifties, bulging chipmunk-like bristled cheeks, a fringe of dark-gray hair around his balding dome, looked up past a customer at her from the cash register. He frowned, nodded to a pay phone at the back by the restrooms and a drinking fountain she would avoid. She worked her way around a hardware counter, stepped past a mop in a bucket of grimy water, and called the sheriff's department number.

"Deputy Clayton," she said when an overworked human being came on the line.

"What you want is the city police," Bob told her when he got on the phone and had asked where she was. "I'll put in the call for you, save you wearing out 911." Esbeth felt a little nervous easing into a similar relationship with city cops. They didn't like outside detectives in the first place, especially amateurs like herself. She expected them to really get their shorts in a bunch when they met her, found she was heading toward her advanced years.

"You weren't calling the cops, were you?" The voice was loud and so close to her that she jumped. Esbeth spun and found the grocer standing very close to her, too close. His teeth seemed amazingly pearly bright and perfect from this close up. The rest of him was less perfect under such close scrutiny.

"Yes," she admitted, "I was."

"They're not coming here, are they?"

"No, to a house down the street. Why?"

His nostrils were twitching like a rabbit yanked out of its warren, his red-rimmed eyes were stretched wide, and his unshaved bulging cheeks were moving in and out, trafficking some breath that said he was a secret smoker. She didn't get the impression that he was attractive up close like that.

"That's all right, then," he said, his eyes lowering. He spun on her, headed back to the counter.

Esbeth didn't have much more time for such jolly entertainment. She went out of J & B's Market and hiked back to Lon's place, at a slow walk this time. Still, she beat the first of the cruisers and the uniforms that began to arrive while she waited outside.

The first cops on the scene swarmed over the place, looking for heaven knew what. The murderer?

A half hour later a tan car with a searchlight on the driver's side pulled up. It had white tax-exempt plates. Two guys climbed out. In case she hadn't figured it out by then, they even looked like plainclothes cops, detectives. The looks on both of them made her want to buy stock in Pepto Bismol—one looked as naturally ugly as homemade sin, and the other looked like a piece of chewed twine.

The taller and slimmer of the two detectives, whose complexion had fought several losing battles long ago, had a scar that ran from the corner of his mouth to his chin. The scar tugged down at the corner of his mouth, gave him a sneer Esbeth suspected he would have worn anyway. He, of course, was in charge. He stood close to Esbeth and ignored her, said to his partner who went inside and came back out, "You get a good look at the stiff?"

"Yeah. Someone sure knocked his receiver off the hook." He looked like his disposition was as sour as his partner's. Esbeth wondered what ever happened to the concept of partnering a good cop with the bad one.

"I'm Sergeant Borster," the tall one said. He didn't hold out a hand or introduce her to his comic relief. "Did you know the deceased?" He had a way of chewing words so that it came out "diseased."

"Long time ago," she said, feeling no encouragement to be windy.

"How long?"

"Twenty years."

Borster's sidekick looked up from the notepad he'd opened, his tongue still poised near the end of a beat-up pencil he had intended to lick.

"You get that, Findlay?" Borster said.

"Yeah." Findlay looked back down and began to scribble.

"What brought you here today," Borster went on, "after twenty years?

"A notion."

"Are you saying that you hadn't seen him in twenty years and that today, of all days, you up and decided to pay him a visit?"

"Well... yeah. Yes, that's about what happened."

"Clarify that."

"Well, I got this note." Esbeth drew it reluctantly from her purse. It was a birthday card, kind of a soupy one at that. She didn't know how anyone else felt about airing their linen, but it was not her thing.

Borster snatched the envelope from her hand, tugged out the card, read from it out loud to Findlay, who scratched along in his notepad.

"Esbeth," Borster read, "I've not treated you right all these years, though I thought about you a lot. I want to make it right with you. I'm going to leave you the house. I've told the family. I hope you'll think better of me. With long-suppressed affection, Lon."

"Whew!" Findlay said, scribbling as fast as he could, although they would probably make a copy of the card later.

Hearing the card's sentiment again, out loud, didn't make Esbeth feel any better about the note.

"He send you a card every year?" Borster asked, folding the card and slipping it back into its envelope.

"No. Just this year. I was surprised, in fact, that he remembered when my birthday was. I came to talk him out of the house part. I didn't want a ding-dong thing from him."

Esbeth glanced around at what she could see of the house as she said it—not much to want anyway. "And I didn't want the sentiment that went with it either," she said.

Findlay looked over the top of his notepad at her in that oily way men did sometimes, like he could look up her skirt and didn't like what he saw there.

"What do you think," Esbeth asked Borster, "that I came here to kill Lon and keep him from giving me a house?"

"Could you repeat that?" Findlay asked.

"Using smaller words this time?"

He looked at Esbeth, his eyes sweeping over her, covering a lot of ground, trying to figure, she guessed, what Lon might have seen in her then if someone old as her had the strength to shove a knife that big up to the hilt in Lonnigan. Esbeth was not too fond of being looked at like that, or in such detail. Years ago she used to say she was inclined toward the voluptuous. Now she just said she cast a firm shadow. Not that she was half a step from getting her own ZIP code or anything, but she was no pixie. No one had called her anorexic lately.

"The guy inside has a piece of brown cloth in his hand," Findlay told Borster. Nothing Esbeth wore was brown. It was not a good color for her.

"I guess we had better talk some more downtown," Borster said to Esbeth.

Chapter 18: Free to Cut to the Chase

Esbeth was still at the police station late that evening, sitting in an interrogation room after answering the same questions over more times than she could count. The bottom line was that she couldn't name a single person who would have any reason to do in poor Lonnie. For all she knew, he had lived alone these past twenty years like Esbeth.

It was Findlay who opened the door finally and said, "You're free to go... for now. Someone's here to pick you up. Hope you didn't have anything else you were supposed to be doing."

"That's the thing about being retired," she said. "You never get any time off."

She was far from best pals yet with these guys. But the guy waiting for her was a friendly and welcome face—Scottie, her photographer pal from the paper, who she had called in her one token phone call.

As soon as they were outside, and Scottie had a Chesterfield going and the passenger door of his car held open for her, he said, "Whoee. Sure don't have to look far for you when a body's found these days, do we."

"I didn't know what a pleasure it was dealing with the sheriff's department," Esbeth grumped, "until I tangled with these city cops. Are they born with an attitude?"

"Big caseload," Scottie said. "I heard Borster wonder out loud why a guy they were working on from a morning case had been shot so many times. Findlay told him, 'Maybe his wife was hard of hearing?'"

"Sounds like an easier one to solve than who did in Lonnigan Saunders." Esbeth told Scottie what she had told the cops, *ad nauseam*, how it had been twenty years since she had even seen Lonnie.

"Yeah, he said you told him once that you happened to be in the neighborhood selling Girl Scout cookies."

"Well, I got tired of the routine."

"You told me about the note, but why *were* you at his house? You coulda called."

It had grown dark outside. The lights of passing cars flickered over them as Scottie drove. The flickers caught for a second in his eyes as he stared at her before looking back to the road.

"We going to my place?"

"Yeah, I had Trent from the paper drive your car over to your place while you were going through the material witness bit so you wouldn't have to fuss with it later. I still got the spare key you loaned me."

"Thanks, Scottie. You're a pal."

"Well?" he said, not going to leave it alone.

She could see that there was no graceful way around it with Scottie. She could stonewall the cops all she wanted. But he had a nose for a story.

"Okay," Esbeth said, "it wasn't just the note. The note was in a card. I didn't tell you that part."

"What kind of card?"

"A birthday card. Today's my birthday," she said. That snapped his head around. "I'm seventy-three."

"How's...?"

She could tell him better than the cold and nasties back at the station. "You know how it is, or maybe you don't. You live like me, alone all your life, and you tell yourself you don't want to make a big fuss because you pass another mile marker. But I was sitting there in my house, the windows open and an autumn breeze blowing through, and it just hit me to go see someone I hadn't seen in a long, long time. To talk with another living soul who might give a hoot. For all the misguided sediment of his sentiment, at least Lon's gesture made me feel linked to something. I was kind of looking forward to seeing him, if only to say no about the house."

"But I was at your house this morning, and you never said…"

"Which is why the windows were open, to clear out the smoke."

He didn't say anything.

"I'm sorry. I was glad you were there. But that was earlier in the day, when I didn't feel like announcing every little…"

"I understand," he said, snuffing out his cigarette and reaching for his pack. Then he stopped himself.

"Go ahead and smoke," she told him. "At least you're not one of those people who think the whole world's a potential ashtray." She had had enough secondary smoke from his company through the years it wasn't going to do her much more damage now, was more than a trade-off for his friendship.

Chapter 19: What Almost Was

"I never told you this," Esbeth said as Scottie got a fresh nail going, "but I almost married Lon. It was a long time ago."

"What happened?"

"It cooled between us. Well, I cooled it, at least once."

He waited, turning a corner with the light. That was the thing about reporters. They'd learned to be good listeners.

"We were kind of high school sweethearts once. But he threw me over for Janie Bigelow, right before prom too." Esbeth could see Scottie squinting at her in the dim light from the street, maybe because of the smoke. "Oh, it wasn't such a big thing. I thought he looked a little too much like his mother then anyway, except for the mustache."

"He never had a mustache."

"His mother did."

"Will you tell this straight?"

"It was a lot of things, hard to understand now. You know," she said, "that time of life is real hard on boys. They've been pals with guys, have buddies on various teams. Suddenly they have to face the concept of becoming best friends with a female, for life. It shakes some of them. The passion business seems to get some of them over the hump. It was that way for Lon, and Janie had more sparkle than me."

"Maybe then."

"Thanks. But my confidence is fine."

"I just..."

"Anyway, he married her, not me."

"Sounds like another case of puppy love that went to the dogs." Scottie pulled up in front of Esbeth's place. As tired as she was, she didn't get right out of the car.

"That was the first time. They eventually got divorced. I was in my sixties by then, about the time when all there is around for pickings are pre-owned spouses. I was wrapping up my teaching in a few years, facing retirement alone. I guess I was restless enough to listen to him for a while. We talked, but this time I turned him down. We'd both changed a lot through the years. I'd gotten too used to living alone, didn't like the way he made living together seem like more of an opportunity to iron his shirts than to have someone to grow old gracefully with. I opted to stay single. He didn't take it well."

"Did he... Was he having money troubles about then too?"

"He was," she admitted. "But that wasn't any part of it." Esbeth had spent a lot of time thinking about that, convincing herself of it.

"And you can't think of anyone who would want to do him harm?"

"Not off the top of my head. But I intend to look into it."

"You know, ol' Lon might have done you a favor after all, given you a birthday present."

"How's that?"

"He couldn't have given someone like you a better present than the challenge of solving his murder."

The next morning, Esbeth kicked off the sheets and charged into the day feeling a whole lot better. Pooped as she had been, she had skipped her evening bath, afraid she'd fall asleep in the tub and wake up an albino prune as she had done in the past. At her age, she didn't need to go out of her way to get more wrinkles.

She didn't linger, though. She had a small pot of coffee, looked through the phone book, and headed down to city hall to look through some records.

It's hard to piece together the life of someone you used to know but haven't been around in a long time—but not impossible. She had a little help in Lonnie's case, since he had spent a little time as a public figure. She picked up a copy of the morning newspaper on her way down to poke through records. Lonnie had made it to the banner story, "Former Mayor Murdered."

Scottie had taken a picture of Lon's place, had had to use a flash. Even with an EMS truck parked in front, it looked spookier than when Esbeth had been there. She raced through the copy, found little hard fact in it about the murder, a lot about Lon's one term as mayor. She headed to a phone outside city hall and got on the horn to Scottie. "Wasn't there one clue at the scene?" she snapped as soon as he was on.

"Clues, you should say," chuckled Scottie. "I never heard of a case with so many clues. Trent's handling the story, but it's the talk of the office. They've got cloth samples, chicken blood in one hallway, a stack of letters from some woman, a mistress they think, who called herself Itchy. No prints, though. And that's just a short dip into the Whitman sampler the cops are working from."

"None of that was in the article."

"Of course not. The heat wants to run out all the leads first, sort through the usual crack-pot confessors. You know how it works. If they can't name any of the hard identifiers, they're bounced out. A case like this brings out all the bedbugs."

"I see Janie is still around."

"And right now she is getting the works from Borster, though I gather she has an iron-clad alibi. I wouldn't go near that man right now, Esbeth, or the house. You may have to work this one from a distance, if you can at all."

"That may be an advantage," she said. "What the cops have to go on sounds like the cowboy who hopped on his horse and rode off in all directions."

"Do you ever wonder what it might be like to have been the wife of the mayor?"

"No," she snapped. Lon's tenure in office was the apex of his career and the beginning of his downward slide. He had been a charmer with a great personality but lacked the single most important quality for leadership. Esbeth's observation, based on teaching school for forty-some years and of surviving life in general, was that the distinguishing characteristic of maturity in any person was the ability to see the big picture. Some kids get it sooner than others, achieve more because they understand the reason for their teachers' assignments. Later they knew all aspects of their job, based on an understanding of several key perspectives. Lon never quite got the handle on that. It showed most when he was put under heavy public scrutiny, was made worse by his only son being killed in a horrible and tragic car accident and his wife carted off to what would today be a Betty Ford clinic, all during his time in office.

He had not only lost his bid for re-election but had gotten so deep in debt that he went bankrupt. It had been a tough time for him, and Esbeth guessed she had been drawn back to him as much as anything by an urge to help him through his tough time. But true to his family trait, he had misunderstood that.

Esbeth hung up and went into city hall, pushed her nose through the records there for a while, then went to the library for a browse. You'd be surprised how much good detecting can be done in a library. She always thought that if she hadn't taught math all those years that she would have liked to have been a librarian. She left there with several pages of notes in her notebook, among them the observation that James Dean had died in 1955, Marilyn Monroe in 1962, Janis Joplin in 1970, and Elvis in 1977. She was one of those folks who, when the path got too obvious, began to poke around for a secondary path, even if it was a stretch.

Since she couldn't get into the murder scene to poke around, she drove over across the river to the newspaper office and had Scottie pull a couple of files from the information morgue for her, He grumbled about being bogged down but kept an eye on her, knew the look she got when she'd caught the whiff of a scent.

Esbeth stared at a pair of clippings for a while until he took the bait and came over to peer over her shoulder.

"What do you know about the Austin music scene?" she said.

He nodded down at one of the clippings, a photo centered in the spread showing Bert Saunders's car, a twisted burning hunk of Detroit's finest wrapped around the cement abutment of a railway overpass. "Should'a had some hot dogs and marshmallows at that one. There wasn't enough of him left to put in a shoebox."

"Was he any good?" Esbeth spared Scottie the look she would normally have shared. Taking pictures like that at accidents didn't make him more callous, but it did generate some defensive mechanisms she'd learn to recognize.

"Some folks called him the next Elvis," Scottie said. "Just as many didn't. He had an LP out that was the hottest thing in town. His group was called Blue Blazes and the Hot Licks at first but was shortened to just Blue Blazes for the recording. They had two more LPs in the can when he died, brought them out posthumously."

"How'd they do?"

"'Bout as well as the biscuits I tried to bake when I was in the service." Scottie looked up, toward his desk where his phone was ringing. "They might have done better with today's recording studio mixing. But they had none of the sizzle of his first one. After a while, even the first LP quit selling. New stars filled the gap."

Esbeth drove to the address she had for Janie, one she had located when she had wrestled loose from looking over the clipping history of Lon's sad tour as mayor. You had to remember that Gerald Ford was president then, hitting his head on doorways and tumbling down airplane steps. A lot of folks who got elected to one public office or another were just a low common denominator, but they usually didn't stay in office very long.

Janie resided in a retirement apartment complex on the far southwest corner of town, where there were some assisted living arrangements. Esbeth drove up a tree-covered hill and got lucky and found a parking place in the shade. She found Janie out by a bed of red and yellow blooming Cannas. A Jacuzzi bubbled all by itself under a gazebo. Janie sat in a wheelchair on the sidewalk beside it. She stared at the bubbles.

"Janie," Esbeth said, a quaver of apprehension in her voice. Visiting folks you knew from childhood, when you'd both lasted to their age, was not always a pure treat.

"Why, Esbeth Walters," she said, looking up. "Is that you?"

"I heard about Lonnie, wanted to see how you've been getting along. Have the police been giving you a hard time?"

"Oh, those men," she waved a fluttery hand, dismissed the bunch of them. "How have you been?" Before Esbeth could answer, Janie said, "It's better here when the sun's out, like now. Better lighting makes for better visibility, don't you think?"

Esbeth gave a slow nod.

"I heard about Lon on the radio. I watch a lot of news on the radio."

"Have you been to see him?"

Janie frowned, shook her frail white head. "Dead people always look so... so dead." Esbeth saw her loose flesh, liver spots, the quiver of her lip, but she was remembering the blond sixteen-year-old she had known so well in school, so full of irrepressible energy, with all the exuberance that attracted boys. Esbeth remembered her as slightly dingy then too. Now Esbeth was starting to get the impression, from the glazy look in her eyes, that these days she might make Gracie Burns look like a rocket scientist by comparison.

"I've been looking into his... death a bit," Esbeth said, "trying to make sense of it. I know the police have asked a lot of questions, but can you remember anything from the time he was mayor that might have come back to haunt him?"

A flicker of real fear scampered across Janie's eyes like a startled animal but was quickly lost somewhere in the sponge of her skull. The blank eyes looked up at Esbeth. "Listen to me slowly," she said. "If you don't succeed in life, you run the risk of failure. It was like that for Lon."

"About your son...?" It was as far as Esbeth got on that.

Janie's eyes snapped open wide, showing little more wisdom than before. "Elvis was by far the greatest living singer," she said, "while he was alive. My boy is... He's..."

Esbeth lost her for a moment. Janie turned and looked into the bubbles, searching for something Esbeth couldn't see when she looked.

"Esbeth," Janie said so abruptly it startled her. "You learn to take the sour with the bitter." She looked up at Esbeth as if seeing her for the first time. "You should marry. An old maid's life is no life for a single woman."

"I don't worry much what other people think," Esbeth said before thinking.

"That's right," she said. "Don't listen to what everyone says, but don't ignore them either."

That was enough of that for Esbeth. She said goodbye and got out of there. She did stop at the complex's clubhouse before leaving, used a phone there to buzz Scottie, tell him what she had in mind, told him where and when to meet her.

Chapter 20: Birthdays Aren't Everyone's Cup of Tea

When Esbeth pulled her car up in front of the J & B's Market that afternoon, she could see the yellow tape around Lon's place down the street. A police cruiser rolled past while she sat there, the cops inside looking over at the house. On the door of the market a sign hung that said, "Back in 20 minutes." She hated signs like that, since they never really said when the person left.

Big splats of rain daubed down across the windshield, here and there, then picked up, and the rain began to come down in earnest, rippling, pounding sheets of it. She looked back toward the store after trying to peer ahead through the windshield. The sign on the door was gone.

She knew she promised Scottie she would wait for him. But it was dark all around the car and ever so lonesome in there. A flash of lightning lit up the street. The crack that split the sky a moment later sounded like it was right on top of her. *Well*, Esbeth figured, *you're never too old to learn something stupid.* She glanced in her purse, pulled a scarf over her head, and shot out the passenger door. She dashed inside the store, ringing the bells on the door as she burst through, dripping, and looking wide-eyed at the proprietor who stood back by the cash register, bent over a spread-out newspaper.

Esbeth gave the man her best drowned-rat grin, tugged off her scarf, and dabbed at her soaked shoulders. He stared at her.

"It's you again," he said.

Esbeth guessed she was not easy to forget. She glanced around the store, all kinds of stuff stacked to the ceiling and around the display gondolas that ran down the center of the store. There were hardware items—nuts and bolts, wrenches, saws—and there were sporting goods: gloves, balls, aluminum Little League bats, and there were pharmaceuticals, candy, magazines. The place had everything. But there was enough dust here and there on the merchandise to convince her that the proprietor wasn't getting rich.

"What do you want?" he said, still on the same theme.

Esbeth edged around a display of some kind of bolts of yard goods, looked ahead to the magazine rack like she was dying for a browse. Where the heck was Scottie?

In spite of all the merchandise, it was a small store and seemed to get smaller as the guy behind the counter began to loom larger behind it.

"You came here for something, didn't you?" He was starting to shout, a trickle of moisture running down from the corner of his mouth. Boy, did this fellow have a low threshold for crowds.

"I... I was hoping to see if you had any tapes... or records... records or tapes of the group Blue Blazes?"

A rumble from outside shook the insides of the little store. Bert moved around from behind the counter, both eyes squinting, his breathing shallow and determined.

Esbeth had seen some renditions of what Elvis might look like if he were alive today. Bert had made some of the same progression since the photos of him as a young rock star, head tilted back, long hair swaying, as lead singer of the group Blue Blazes.

"The police probably want to talk with you," Esbeth said. "They'll be as surprised as everyone else when they hear you aren't dead. The store, you know, is registered in your mother's name, part of the settlement. Imagine, you're living right here close all these years, you and your father seeing each other almost daily. You boiling with a steady, maybe increasing resentment at a scheme that didn't pan out, finally exploding when you thought Lon was going to cheat you out of a run-down house like that. I'm sure that once they know what they're looking for, the police will be here quick as stink on a dead skunk."

He lunged and grabbed for her. Esbeth was expecting it and darted back around the far end of the counter. She was quicker than folks expected of an old coot like her, for short stretches. She hoped this race wasn't going to go the distance.

"You know," she said conversationally while sprinting in the other direction as he dashed around the far end of the center display gondola after her then stood there panting and staring at her a moment, "I understand you thinking that if you faked your death that your work might sell better than ever, like Elvis, Marilyn, James Dean. But I hear the two LPs released weren't that hot, and you were no looker back then. Even Janis was better looking. In those days, at your best, you looked like seven miles of bad road."

Like she expected, he shot down the aisle after her. Esbeth pulled over the bolts of yard goods and raced to the back of the store, stood behind the cash register, watched him tumble over the bolts of cloth, and land in some nasty-sounding buckets and rakes. The phone began to ring. She hoped that wasn't Scottie calling to say he'd be late.

Bert scrambled to his feet, hair sticking out—what there was of it—a small cut on his forehead bleeding down into one eye. He stood fiddling with something at the door.

At Esbeth's age, she didn't have many of these wind sprints in her. She'd pretty well played her hand on the heavy running, probably shouldn't have said what she said next. "This isn't all about one of those midlife crisis things you men go through, is it?"

He raced the length of the store, dove clear over the counter, grabbed at her, and fell over the top of the counter that crashed over after him, the cash register falling to the floor beside him or on him. Esbeth didn't get a close look, having faked right, slipped left, shoved the bucket and mop back there at him, and scurried out of reach toward the front of the store.

Esbeth bent over, breathing hard herself now as he crawled out from under the splintered wood and broken glass. She reached for the door, found it locked. So that was what he'd been doing.

"Why'd you have to kill him?" Esbeth said. "Your own father? Was it just resentment that he spent what music money you'd made on the lottery of politics? Or was it the house? If you'd just left him alone, I'd have turned down his offer. Now the police will find out you're alive, and they'll figure past all that rubbish you left as clues. They aren't dolts, you know." True to his family trait, he hadn't dwelt on consequences then, or Esbeth guessed, now.

All the planting he'd done of dummy clues would stack up against him as premeditation. Maybe he did know it, didn't care. He'd picked up a knife somewhere in the back of the store and was stalking her way.

Esbeth gave up on the door, sidled around the counter, keeping as much space between them as possible.

"There's one simple thing you didn't seem to get when you were a young sprat, don't seem too much closer to now," Esbeth said, panting. "And that is that respect is a two-way street. Life's as simple as that if you..."

He shot around the end of the counter and charged. Esbeth was too pooped to run any more. She knocked over everything she could reach. He barely stumbled as he clambered through the mess coming at her. Without thinking, Esbeth reached around, snatched up one of those aluminum ball bats, whirled it around, and conked him squarely on the forehead as he lunged the last few inches toward her.

You wouldn't believe the awful *thonk!* it made as it connected. She didn't know whether his eyes crossed or not. But she heard him fall as she moved in the other direction as fast as she could go, which was no land speed record. She heard a steady thumping and pounding, glanced back. It wasn't coming from Bert. He was catching a little power nap of his own, curled up in the debris. The noise was coming from the door.

She worked her way through the mess they'd made of the store, opened the double latches she had only fumbled with before. Scottie, Trent, Sergeant Borster, and Findlay all rushed inside.

Scottie stood by her while the others rushed to Bert. "I'd have been here sooner," he said, "but I stopped first to chat with Borster."

"It was a bust," Esbeth told Scottie, opening her purse to show the tape player still turning. "I didn't get a confession, just my own ranting."

"Don't need it," Borster called out from where they were clamping cuffs on Bert and easing him upright. He blinked and looked confused at the cops holding him. "If you had just shared with us what you told these guys from the local squeak, we would have handled everything. That's our job, you crazy old—"

"Go easy," Scottie said softly.

Borster gave him a look but shut up. He and Findlay tugged Bert toward the police car outside, its red and blue lights sweeping in sparkling lines through the downpour. "Meet us at the station," he called back to Scottie and Esbeth. "We still need your statements."

It was kind of quiet there in the store as the cruiser pulled away in the rain. Trent nonchalantly pulled a Mars bar from the candy rack and began to open it.

"The teeth are what put me on to him in the first place," Esbeth said to no one in particular. She was still pumped full enough of adrenaline to be talkative. She could bet she'd sleep well tonight. "They weren't false and were too perfect for someone like him who hadn't been in show business once."

"Man," Trent said, "I sure hope I'm around when you're a hundred."

"There's no reason you shouldn't be," Esbeth said, still panting, "if you watch your health."

Scottie fired up a Chesterfield, looked at her with that raised-eyebrow look of his. He said, "Looks like you took full advantage of that birthday gift Lon left you."

"Well," Esbeth said, "that's all good and fine. But I wish he'd wrapped it better."

Chapter 21: Who Killed the Bride?

The tiny blond flower girl had her finger up her nose. The ring bearer stood pulling at the seat of his pants. A gentle hum of voices above the organ music said that the natives as well as the rest of the wedding attendees were getting restless.

Corrine Sandlebee, who sat next to Esbeth, much closer than she needed to be, whispered to her, "Why do you do it, Esbeth? Get tangled up in solving things the police should be handling? Murders and such."

Esbeth could have told her that the police didn't always solve them, had far more work on their plates than they needed. But she told her a deeper truth, one about herself. "It keeps me young," she admitted. "As long as I can grow, keep learning, it sorta peps me up. I need that."

They sat in the Q-tip row of the wedding party. Esbeth, in her early seventies, was not the oldest one of them. On a trip to Florida once, she'd heard some whippersnapper or other refer to the tiny white head of hair that barely stuck up at the steering wheel of the yellow Cadillac ahead of them as a "cue tip." The way some folks drove down there, especially ones from her set—it was no wonder folks had come up with names for them. She saw a lot of short-attention-span accidents while there, which made her a more cautious driver.

"I mean, land, Esbeth, isn't it risky?"

The tall wooden doors at the back of the church swung open at last and not a moment too soon. Esbeth had seen a lot of heads in the wedding party turning back that way, a lot of glancing at watches. These things were often slow to launch, but this one was sure burning a long fuse.

The organist caught the gentle bang of wood, switched gears in a practiced segue to "Here Comes the Bride." But instead of the bride and her father, Ira Burgess came running out of the vestibule, yelled to the whole assembly, "She's dead. Someone's killed her!"

The crowd began to spill out of the pews, in small clumps at first then in a general outpouring. The organ playing stuttered to a stop. The hum of voices in the room grew much louder, lanced here and there by a shout or scream.

Esbeth didn't know the wedding families all that well. Corrine had talked her into going to this one with her, but Esbeth didn't mind all that much. Weddings were good for oldsters, she figured. They left her with a feeling of hope, a sense that there was a future, the kind of feeling she got from watching a vigorous farmer plant a crop in the spring. That is, except when the bride was knocked six ways from Sunday and was lying sprawled and dead across the steep front steps of the church, where folks couldn't help seeing her as they crowded out past where young Laney Richards lay halfway down the stairs, her white dress spread out like the wings of a fallen bird.

There was always a lot of emotion at a wedding. For that matter, there was usually a lot of emotion involved in a violent murder. But there was an excess load at the moment. From where she stood at the top of the stairs by the doors, Esbeth could see that the groom, Trandt Michaels, stood mid-stairs and held a wrought iron cowboy boot doorstop high in the air by its toe, waving it. One end of it looked bloody. He was trying to scream and cry at the same time. He tossed the boot aside and dropped to his knees on the steps beside Laney. A couple of the older men stepped closer and kept him from moving the body, and that turned into a wrestling match.

Esbeth could have told Trandt, if he was fit to listen to reason, that the cops were going to be sore enough with him for handling that doorstop, would have really come down on him if he had jostled the body. As it was, the others led him away and had him sit down off to one side on the grass now where a small group of men stood around him. His hair was tousled, greased enough to stand out in strands. His shoulders shook as he sobbed. He tugged with nervous hands at his wrinkled tuxedo.

Esbeth looked down where the matching boot doorstop had been moved back into its place, holding open its door. On the side, where the other boot had stood, there was a black mark, like a small skid. As she went down the stairs, she eased to the far side from where the body lay. Once down, she stayed as close as she could to the stairs, which was hard, what with everyone crowding in, trying to get a peek without seeming too obvious about it.

Laney lay facedown on the stairs, her head pressed against the concrete steps, the long train of her dress wrapped around one leg. It wasn't hard to imagine she was dead. Blood was mixed in some of the splayed strands of her long red hair, and a small pool had formed a step down from her. Esbeth noticed she had a tattoo on one ankle, thought it might be of a unicorn at first, then saw it was a Harley Davidson emblem as she stood on tiptoe to see. She also wore a slim gold ankle bracelet on that leg. *Kids these days!*

Esbeth stood blinking in the sun, wishing it was still those times when they wore bonnets, or at the least hats. She sensed a presence beside her and looked up to see the young preacher standing next to her with a slightly open mouth, staring at the fallen girl.

"She's not... She's not..."

"Going to get up," Esbeth said.

The preacher looked down at Esbeth, eyes barely connecting, certainly not recognizing her. She'd never seen him before. He was a young one, barely in his twenties. Corrine had told Esbeth that he'd only started preaching at the church a year back. The congregation was still adjusting to him. He looked nice enough. Short, neat hair, a wholesome farm-raised face, one of those black silk gowns like a choir robe, black slacks, and black Rockport Walkers on his feet. Esbeth gave him extra points for common sense in wearing comfortable shoes. A young preacher was going to get lots of exercise if he was going to shepherd a flock as active as this one was turning out to be. Two men had squared off outside the circle of folks gawking at Laney and waiting for the law to arrive. They were shouting and waving arms at one another. The preacher started then moved over toward them. He moved slowly, with a slight limp. Esbeth tagged along.

One of the combatants was short, had reddish hair close to Laney's in tone. His face was almost as red as he hopped around, banty rooster style, circling the bigger man, yelling up at him. "The way I raised her had nothing to do with harsh discipline."

The big dark-haired man with silver temples wasn't backing down. "You might have been a little more strict."

"Beat her the way you did Trandt at every little excuse?"

"Now, now," the preacher beside Esbeth said too softly for anyone to hear.

"You calling me violent?" the big man boomed. "I'll smash in your face for calling me that."

"How can you? How can you?" a woman screamed at them. Esbeth glanced her way, saw it was Trandt's mother, remembered it couldn't be Laney's mother. She had died a long time back.

"The groom was supposed to be with me, in my office," the preacher said. This time enough people heard him. Heads swung toward his quiet voice. "But he wasn't. Said he was feeling ill, went to the restroom. The usual bachelor party hijinks, I figured."

The big man's face was fixed on the preacher now. He took a step the guests' way, ignoring Laney's father, who still circled him, shouting. "What are you saying?" His voice was full of sinister threat.

"Now Bert," his wife said. She was a mousy woman, whose voice, far from calming Bert, seemed to affect him like a cheerleader egging him on.

The preacher took a halting step back as Bert advanced. "Ask the boy. He'll tell you that…"

As the heads in the crowd swung in Trandt's direction, they merely located another eye of the hurricane. Trandt was squared off against his best man, holding him by the lapels of his tux and shaking him. "What are you blubbering about, Karey? What was she to you?"

"Look, she wasn't always a saint or something," Karey mumbled through the tears, not resisting. "You knew that."

"It's *my* baby she was carrying, after all."

"You don't *know* that. She told *everyone* that."

"She told you that?" Stark incredulity showed in every word Trandt shouted.

"Yeah. But I wasn't the only…"

Trandt rattled Karey harder, his best man's head snapping forward and back. Karey made no effort to raise a hand to defend himself.

"But you," Trandt screamed. "Why you?" He continued to rattle Karey like a cocktail shaker. A carnation flew off Karey's jacket and got trampled as folks crowded close to the two of them.

"It wasn't just me," Karey sputtered. "I'm trying to tell you. You had to know. Didn't you know?"

A few seconds ago Karey had been one of those holding Trandt away from the body. Tears shone on his cheeks in the bright sun as his bobbing head whipped back and forth as Trandt shook him.

Bert charged through the crowd, jostled people to the left and right, shoved his thick arms between the boys, and knocked Trandt loose and back. The groom landed on the seat of his tux pants for the second time. He sat there glaring up at his father.

The first cruiser chose that moment to pull up to the curb, an EMS vehicle right behind it. Two uniformed cops tumbled out of the police car and came sprinting over to the huddle of panting and glaring men, began to separate them. An unmarked police car wheeled up, parked at a jutting angle to the curb. Esbeth flinched as Sergeant Borster got out of the passenger side, his sidekick Findlay from the driver's side. She made herself small as they strode over to the throng, full of purpose and bad attitude.

"Land's sake, Esbeth," a shrill voice beside her said, far too loud for Esbeth's taste. It was Corrine. "Where did you get off to? I was ready to…"

The preacher sidled into the middle of things, met the detectives, who brushed by him and went to have a look at Laney.

"This new shepherd for your flock," Esbeth said to Corrine, "Is he…?"

"He's just fine." Esbeth could swear the biddy was blushing as she ogled in his direction. "Some young thing's going to…"

"How can you?" Esbeth snapped. "At a time like this." Several of the young women in the crowd *had* been giving the young preacher a studied eye, a smile when he looked their way.

"Why's he limping?" Corrine said. "He never…" But something else caught her eye.

"Look at that, will you?" She bent closer, gave Esbeth a nudge. Esbeth followed the path of her stare and saw Laney's older sister, Anna, beside Ira Burgess, the maid of honor. Anna had dissolved into deep gulping sobs. She stared up at where the detectives bent over her sister.

"I'll bet they have some questions for *her*," Corrine said in a sotto voce whisper. "Oh, she's sorry now. But I hear that at the rehearsal dinner, she made quite a scene, jumped up in the middle of dinner, knocking over her chair, and screamed that Laney would get married first over Anna's dead body or her own."

"Corrine," Esbeth said, "you're a gossip."

Corrine was still staring down at Esbeth, mouth pursed and neck stuck up stiff when Esbeth got a familiar whiff of Chesterfield smoke. She spun and spotted Scottie elbowing through the crowd with his camera.

He winked at her, said past the cigarette hanging from his lip, "First wedding I ever been to that could get a featured in *Ring* magazine."

Esbeth could see back in the crowd through which he'd just pushed his way that some of the men had a grip on Bert and were holding him struggling in place while Laney's father still shouted at him. Another group worked to keep the groom and best man apart.

When she turned back around, Scottie had made it to the stairs, got the sign from the cops to take a few shots. Scottie worked for the newspaper daily, and she knew they wouldn't print any of the close-ups he was taking now, would provide them to the police as a courtesy, would probably print nothing more gripping than a body bag being lifted into the EMS vehicle.

Chapter 22: Something Blue

Esbeth saw that the medical examiner's assistant had joined the men on the stairs. They were working quickly now, wanting to get to that bag stage before any of the electronic media arrived and got their handheld cameras rolling. Esbeth, for one, wasn't anxious to see a film at eleven on this one either. A couple of the other cops were struggling to get the heavy bloody doorstop into a large evidence bag without touching it.

More uniformed officers arrived. They began herding everyone into a lump on the lawn. Borster stood and turned to the crowd, boomed at them, "Don't anyone leave. We want to talk to everyone before you go." A few groans came from the crowd. It was over a hundred degrees out there in the sun and with no promise of lemonade either.

Esbeth shook herself loose from Corrine, weaseled her way up through the crowd where Findlay had already started on a few of the principals. What with all the shouting and crowd chatter, it was hard to catch more than a word or two at first. She squinted and concentrated.

"Just the three of us, Mickey, that's Laney's dad, her, and me in the vestibule," she heard Ira Burgess telling him, "and she spun on us and shot out the door. Mickey wanted to follow her, but I told him, 'Give her a minute. It's just the jitters.'" She sniffed as she talked, wiping at tears that were starting all over again. "But then... But then the next time I ever saw her she was..."

"Where in the dickens did you get to?" Corrine shouted, grabbing at Esbeth's arm like she was her lost child. "I've been looking all over for..."

Esbeth tried to push around her and get in a position to listen, but Corrine wasn't having any of it. She finally sensed what Esbeth was up to, said, "You're not thinking of trying to get involved, are you?" Esbeth felt herself flush at the scolding voice, took a couple of deep breaths before she spoke.

"We *are* involved," she said. "Now, if you'll get out of my ding-dong way..."

"Well, I never, in all my born days."

Esbeth shook off her clutch and ducked under an outstretched arm and got closer again. Borster had come over to stand beside Findlay at the bottom of the stairs. The preacher stood next to him. The EMS crew was lifting the bag onto a stretcher just as two vans from competing television crews pulled up and began to shout and pull equipment from their trucks.

Findlay was talking with Karey, whose shirt was ripped and missing a stud, his tie untied and hanging loosely around his open collar. In spite of the little fracas he'd just had with Trandt, he did the groom a huge favor. Esbeth heard him tell Findlay, "Trandt was with me the whole time. He was down in the head having a bout of dry heaves. Last night we..."

The preacher pushed forward, started to say something. Borster tugged him back to his side. "Get all these people over into the parking lot," Borster snapped at one of the men in uniform.

"There's something..." The preacher had stepped forward again.

"What?" Borster spun and snapped, staring at the preacher.

The uniformed cops were herding the crowd. One of the advantages of age, Esbeth always figured, was that you could act dotty now and again in short stretches. She acted as if she was turning to follow the others then wandered back and around in time to be close enough to hear the preacher say, "It's important."

Borster just nodded. Findlay turned to listen too.

"What I was trying to tell you," the preacher said, "was that when I went to look for the groom, I stuck my head outside the back stairs of my office. I could see the street from there and saw a motorcycle pull up at the curb in front of the church. The man wore a leather jacket, shouted something. I saw a flutter of white at the front of the church. It might have been the bride rushing out. But I had to look back in on the congregation, the wedding party inside. They were getting restless."

"Borster," Esbeth said, loudly enough to be heard. She hadn't realized that the uniformed cops had the rest of the crowd over in the parking lot by now, that she kind of stood out there alone on the lawn anyway. One of the cops was just coming back over after her.

"Esbeth Walters," Borster said in more of a snarl than a greeting. "That's what we need. Look, Findlay, at who's here to solve the case for us. Guess you can put away your notebook."

Findlay grinned at Esbeth, looking more than a little like a hyena smiling up from a fresh kill. The others from the close families still gathered in a knot by the police stared at the little old lady getting the razz from the sergeant. Scottie was there. He was grinning, too, but his grin was different from Findlay's.

Borster didn't leave it alone. "You going to tell us who did it? Give us the murderer on a plate? I suppose you know the biker..."

"There wasn't any biker," Esbeth said, biting her tongue to keep from adding, "you ninny."

"Who...?" Findlay said.

"Yeah." Borster's tone was at its snide best. "Who did do it, then? Who should we collar?"

"Him," Esbeth said, pointing at the preacher.

Every head snapped the preacher's way, and Esbeth had to give him credit. His face was as close to the unjustly accused as one could get. Before he could say anything, feisty little Mickey Richards pushed forward shouting, "All those visits to the house. You said you were counseling her. But you never thought I knew just how much, did you?"

"She should never have worn white," Anna said, looking up from her blubbering.

Borster squinted at the preacher.

"He's been pitting everyone against each other out here," Esbeth shouted, keeping the momentum going, "has changed his story a couple of times. But he's the only one who had time to come around the building, try to talk Laney out of the wedding at the last moment. Probably tripped over that doorstop in the shuffle. But he did leave a mark from his shoe where it sat, probably stubbed his toe in the scuffle. That mark will match the rubber from his sole if you check."

The preacher shook his head vigorously, had somehow lost the ability to speak. He took a limping and telling step backward, looked from face to face with a pleading look.

"The fall might have even been an accident," Esbeth said. She had their attention now. Everyone in their little group was quiet but her. She could hear the mumbling chatter of the crowd a ways from them. "I don't even think the doorstop was the murder weapon. She may have fallen hard and wrong down the stairs, tripping in the tangle of her train, the way it was wrapped around one leg. He probably knocked the doorstop that far when he tumbled over it rushing to get back around to the other side of the church, knocked it into the blood that formed a pool. The medical examiner can confirm some of this. The only prints you'll probably find on the doorstop belong to Trandt."

"I... I... didn't mean..." The preacher seemed torn between grabbing at the out of an accidental death or staying with his original bluff. Instead of either, he spun and tried to make a limping run but got no farther than into the arms of Bert, who grabbed him in a bear hug. That didn't stop Trandt from stepping in close, trying to take a feeble swing at the squirming preacher. Karey and Mickey stepped in and pulled him back.

The lights of the television crews flicked on in unison, began to record the last sad scene in detail.

"Get him out of here," Borster yelled.

Findlay and a couple of the uniformed men tugged the preacher loose from Bert's grip and hustled him toward one of the police cars. The preacher's head turned back toward them. He shouted, "The Lord is my shepherd..." putting on a show for the gallery in the parking lot, many of whom were calling out, asking what was going on. They surged against the uniformed men, who held them back as they watched the preacher get loaded into the back of the car.

"You'd better come down to the station, too, Esbeth," Borster sighed to Esbeth. "We're going to need your statement." He stalked off toward his car.

Scottie was busy snapping pictures, getting knocked about a bit by the television crews in the process. He came back over to her in a few minutes after the flashing lights of the last cruiser had pulled away. Some of the people milled about, consoling the members of the family who were all crying now. Others got in their cars and drove away. Corrine came bustling toward Esbeth, a real bee in her bonnet this time.

"Esbeth," she snapped, "I hope you haven't been making a pest out of yourself. Wherever are they taking the preacher? He's such a nice young man. The young ladies are just sick."

"I never thought I'd find you here when I caught the squeal for this one on the scanner," Scottie said from her other side. He shared a Cheshire smile while reaching for the pack in his shirt pocket. "What say we go somewhere and grab an ice cream?"

"Might as well," Esbeth said. "I've had all the dose of getting a feeling of hope for the future here I want for now."

"Well, you can just find your own way home," Corrine huffed. She held her nose up and tilted her head back as she spun away from Esbeth. "You'd just be getting our choir director or the organist hauled in for something if you stayed here."

Chapter 23: Remembering Maine

Esbeth sat up straight in the wooden rocker as a loon cried out its long mournful call from far across the other side of a dark lake. That is plain out one of the eeriest and most macabre sounds you'll ever hear, she thought. It sounded like the noise a small child might make when an arm was being pulled slowly from a socket.

Chills shot in electric ripples up and down Esbeth's back.

The still, cool air around the cabin porch seemed deathly quiet, except for a chirp or two from a bug and the creaking of their wooden rockers on the half-loose wooden boards of the porch.

The haunting sound yanked Esbeth away from the point she had been trying to make, which had something to do with the roll sideways through life that their friend Mary Elizabeth had been through.

"I still think Mary Elizabeth should ought to have come along," Abby insisted. "I mean, she planned the whole outing."

"It's been just wonderful up here too," Garlena said, and she didn't sound like she was trying to be facetious, though it was in her to be so. "Think how dry and hundred-degree hot it is back in Texas right now."

"Hot enough for chickens to be dancing the Charleston just to keep their drumsticks in the air," Esbeth said.

Abby nodded. "Ranchers'll be burning the needles off cactus just so the cattle can have some moisture. Many's the time I've empathized with those panting steers at this time of year."

The three of them wore flannel shirts, and Garlena and Abby had sweaters and shawls handy. None of them were young. Each had hair as white as a Q-tip. Esbeth felt like her bones were close to the surface in this sort of chill air.

"The beasts of the field aside," Abby said, "it still seems a shame Mary Elizabeth couldn't put her feelings aside and come along any old way."

"Maybe *she's* glad, though," Garlena said.

"You mean 'cause Noreen's along?" Abby said. "But they were getting to be close friends again and after lo these many years."

"*Were*," Garlena emphasized. "That Bert Carson!" She didn't need to explain to Esbeth and Abby that he'd been like a boil at Mary Elizabeth's side then had up and quit paying attention to her and started nosing around Noreen right after Jimmy Dolan's death.

"Jimmy was courting Noreen a dozen years, right up until they were in their eighties, and then he had to go and pop off," Abby said. "Heart just went boom."

Garlena nodded. "Bert dumping her sure must've gotten Mary Elizabeth's tail up over her back."

"Now, Garlena," Abby said, "you know the Good Book says we shouldn't judge others, though I do admit we all have to sort through the facts now and again." They all knew, though, that she was almost always the first in line to judge anyone.

"You put a handy spin on that," Garlena said.

Esbeth tuned them out for a moment and concentrated on the cool black night around them, so different from August back in Austin, from where they all hailed. In spite of enjoying the sights and temperature of Maine, all day she had been feeling every bit of her advanced years, something she usually didn't do, or admit to if she did. Though they had walked about only a bit that day, she had felt an ache growing in her right hip—one of those piercing, stabbing pains like a rusty knife going into and twisting at the ball of her right hip. She'd hobbled to and from the dining area, plopped at last into the rocker, pulled a lap rug over her, and planned to stay there as long as she could, even though the cool had been creeping in while the light faded.

Abby, Garlena, and Esbeth all sat on their wooden rockers on the wooden porch the way folks used to, talking—the way most people were too busy to do anymore. But when you were in your senior years, as they all were, you found time to talk. The air was cool, and there was a pine-smelling rustling little breeze that swept across them. It was August, but the first frost was going to be on the pumpkin real soon around this corner of America.

Shanna bustled across from the cabin next door, went inside the cabin Esbeth shared with Abby, never said a word to them, and just rustled around in there doing something. Esbeth could hear her moving chairs and tossing stuff around.

"Odd," Garlena said. The three of them were all about the same age, while Shanna was a mere child, barely forty. She was Garlena's great-niece and had come along because of boy trouble at home. The trouble was that she didn't know any.

Since she was so different from the white-haired rest of them, Esbeth had spent time thinking about her. She was very slender and had long witch-black hair and a few mannerisms that made her fit in with the rest of them better than she should have. Esbeth had never seen such a young person so ready for older age. All her nesting instincts seemed aimed at a graceful retirement someday. Earlier on the trip, Garlena had wondered out loud to Esbeth why Shanna was still single at her age. Speaking just for herself, Esbeth didn't wonder about it at all.

Shanna came out of the cabin, letting the screen door bang behind her. It was cool out, but she didn't wear so much as a sweater. She didn't look at any of them again this time and walked right past them back toward the cabin she was sharing with Noreen.

"Stranger and stranger," said Garlena.

Esbeth wished that Noreen was out on the porch with them. She was the one of them Esbeth had been most eager to spend time with when she was first talked into filling in for Mary Elizabeth and coming on the trip. Noreen and Esbeth had been best friends in high school. That wasn't in the Stone Age or anything, but sometimes it felt like it. They both lived in Austin, though they never seemed to find time to spend with each other. Esbeth had been really looking forward to catching up. But Noreen had been feeling a bit puny and had begged off to lie down a spell.

The others had droned on. Esbeth realized she hadn't been paying much attention for a while and had been listening more to the rustle of the pines than what the others had to say. She only knew they had stopped. She caught the direction they were staring, swung her head that way, and found that Shanna was once more amongst them. Shanna stood on the edge of the porch, looking pale and wide-eyed. Her hands twisted with each other in front of her. Her voice, when she spoke, lacked its usual practiced huskiness, was instead brittle enough to break like a crust of ice. What she finally did say fit with the cool dark night in the same eerie way as the call of the loon earlier.

"What's good for getting blood out of a rug?" she said. "A lot of blood."

Esbeth blinked more than once and looked at Shanna more closely, expecting to see a grin spread across her face. Esbeth's wooden rocker slowed to a creaking jerky halt on the wooden porch as she stared instead at a face as ashen white as her own hair. The girl was clearly in shock. As her words sank in, so was Esbeth.

"Noreen?" Esbeth said.

Shanna's head moved up and down in a way almost too rigid and out of control to be called a nod.

Oh, land.

Esbeth pushed herself slowly to her feet, tried to stand, but it took two pushes to get herself upright. Then she tried to hurry after Shanna. But the hip didn't kick right in. It chose to not work and throb instead. She had to ease it into the idea of forward movement.

"Come on," Shanna urged, waving at Esbeth to follow faster.

She pushed past the bursts of color caused by the pain in her hip as she hobbled after Shanna as fast as she could. The more she walked, the better she could go. But it wasn't anything she would have chosen to do without the urgency of a crime drawing her.

At the doorway, Shanna paused, and they went through together. Noreen lay sprawled across the throw rug in front of the black Franklin stove that heated their cabin. Shanna had not been wrong about the blood. It was everywhere, and there was far too much of it for there to be any hope for Noreen. Esbeth glanced at her watch, saw it was 8:20 p.m. Every night at 10:30 p.m., the people who ran the lodge turned off their gas-burning generator, and that was lights-out for everyone unless you had candles or wanted to try to read by a kerosene lantern.

"Where's Bo Emma?" Esbeth asked.

"Still over at the lodge. She went back for another piece of pie she said she didn't have room for after supper. Noreen gave it a miss, and you were kind of..."

"Crabby?" Esbeth said. Well, it was true. "We all have our days," she said with a sigh. "We'd better get on over to the lodge while everyone's still up and the power's on."

Seeing Noreen lying there dead still hadn't sunk in all the way for Esbeth yet. She felt numb as they wove through the trail to the lodge. She was wishing she'd thought to grab a sweater or bring along the lap rug, even though she wore heavy jeans with her flannel shirt.

With the possible exception of wanting to find a bathroom and not being able to, there was nothing worse than being in the mood to go to bed and not being able to. But it looked like the lodge would run the generator longer than usual tonight, and they'd all be up for a while.

Then her amateur detective side's eagerness let up, and it finally got all the way through to Esbeth that Noreen was the one lying dead back there in that wide pool of blood. Esbeth's regret started with some of the stupid little things she wished she'd told Noreen. Esbeth stopped where she stood, still halfway up the gravel and stone walk to the lodge.

"Come on," Shanna called to her. In the distance behind them, Esbeth could make out Abby and Garlena talking loudly and coming their way.

Esbeth looked up from the dim path to Shanna, could barely see her. Esbeth's eyes misted over, and she stood there shaking, racked with sobs, feeling as useless as she'd ever felt in her life.

"I don't know *what* killed her," Esbeth said into the only phone at the lodge. "No. Nor who. Yeah, it *does* seem like murder. Well, I don't know what'll happen. Sure, I'll let you know." She hung up the receiver, straightened the phone on its corner of the lobby desk.

The lodge's dining area was part of the biggest building at the lodge. The office was in a corner as guests entered the building, next to the adjacent game room and library. The kitchen was off behind that. The red-and-white-checkered-tablecloth-covered dining tables occupied the main portion of the room, while along one wall was a fireplace so big that it could burn a four-foot piece of log. There was even a small self-service bar if you had brought your own spirit adjuster. The building was made of hewn logs like the smaller cabins that fanned around the lodge facing the lake. The walls were lined with knotty pine and various trophies—mounted fish and the heads of bigger game, deer, bear, and moose. As Esbeth looked up from the desk, every stuffed critter's glass eyes seemed to stare at her in fixed curiosity.

She went back out to the table where the round shape of Bo Emma sat with a fork poised over a plate. Esbeth doubted from the Pillsbury look of her that she really needed any more pie, but she understood the nervous energy that made her want to keep her hands busy.

"How'd Mary Elizabeth take it?" Bo Emma asked as Esbeth sat back down. Shanna and Abby sat at another table with one of the deputies who had come along with the Aroostook County Sheriff.

"About like we're all taking it," Esbeth said, "on the hard side." She glanced to the far corner of the lodge hall where the staff and guests were being interviewed by the law. Garlena was being interviewed at the moment.

When it was Esbeth's turn, the lodge manager, Lamant Willis, came over to the table. He nodded at her and jerked his head, with its closely cropped white hair, toward the corner table by the fireplace. If Lamant was on a word budget, he was sure ahead of the mark since they'd arrived. Even the current hubbub hadn't brought out his windy side. He walked with his stiff slumped shoulders over to where he'd been puffing on a pipe at a table by himself. He sat flexing his hands and looking down at them, the way a man his age would, as if surprised he could still use them at all. His knuckles were swollen in an arthritic way. He had to be at least Esbeth's age. His ears were long, as was his face. He had a familiar look to Esbeth, but then most people who had arrived at her age always did.

Esbeth looked across the red-and-white-checked tablecloth at Bo Emma, who was picking at her piece of blueberry pie. Their eyes met, and Bo Emma struggled for an encouraging look. Her usually beaming round face was, for the first time Esbeth could recall, not smiling. The thing about Bo Emma, as her former mother-in-law, Mary Elizabeth, once told Esbeth, was that we all have anatomy, but some of us just wear ours differently. One feature Bo Emma had a lot of was anatomy. At a mere 41 years, she seemed reconciled to going through life as a plus size. At the moment she was filling out—and Esbeth could see that meant filling—an outfit, tan on tan, that could well be from Abercrombie & Fitch—if it was the fishing and sporting side of the company. But Esbeth had no real room to talk. If she ever posed for a Victoria's Secret catalog, there was going to be a whole new secret. As it was, Esbeth shared what feeble grin she could with Bo Emma and was sorry not to get a grin back. Esbeth could have used some of her usual cheeriness about now.

Esbeth pushed herself up from the captain's chair and, feeling creaky, made her way across the room as best she could. It was a little after midnight, and yet the lights were on in the lodge. The sound of the nearby generator running hummed in the otherwise still night. Each small table had been covered with the same red and white checkered cloths as the one Sheriff Milen Baxter sat behind. Esbeth sat down in the chair across from him.

He looked up from a worn notebook into which he had been scribbling. "Is this your first murder?" Esbeth asked.

"I fear not, Miss…" He looked down at his notebook. "Walters." He looked back up at her. He was a younger, leaner man than she'd expected. Like most other native men she'd seen so far, he wore a checkered flannel shirt. He looked more like a game warden than the lawmen she was used to, but his eyes fit the model—the way they looked right into her, turning over rocks. They were an honest ice-water blue in the weather-leathered tan of his face. His hair was straight and sandy blond, a lock of it hanging down in a sweep across his forehead. He had some Viking blood in him, she guessed. On first inspection, Esbeth placed him as one of those men who in the dead of winter would know just what to do if left in the woods with no provisions. He would survive, and he would be someone you could trust your life to if you were among that abandoned party. Of course, that was all gut response, but she liked and trusted what she saw.

"You the medical examiner up here too?" Esbeth asked.

"No. The state has one. He'll be here by tomorrow morning. I flew in ahead from Caribou," he said.

Esbeth guessed she disappointed him by not telling him his arms sure must be tired.

His smile was warm and genuine. "You're still a bit in shock, aren't you?"

She nodded. "Tired too," she admitted. He seemed so young—hard to tell how much experience he had.

"The woman..."

"Victim," Esbeth said. "It's all right."

"Noreen Dolan. She was a friend of yours?"

"My best friend. Well..."

"You were going to say."

"I mean she used to be my best friend. But she'd been married a long time. We hadn't been as close for a while. But I'd hoped on this trip we could fix that."

He didn't say anything when Esbeth choked up, just gave her a moment or two. Then he said, "How did you come to be on this outing?"

It was a good question. Esbeth didn't know how much he knew so far. She said, "Another lady was supposed to have come, Mary Elizabeth. But she..."

"Go on."

"She decided not to come, asked me to come in her place."

"And?"

"I've had better outings," Esbeth admitted. "It's been a long hot summer back in Austin. I thought Maine would be a pleasant change. It *has* been cool and beautiful up here, but there are times I've felt better. And... like I said, I was hoping to get to spend time with Noreen, catch up on old times."

"There are two bedrooms in each of the cabins," he said. "But you and the late Mrs. Dolan, Noreen, were in different cabins. Any reason for that?"

Esbeth sighed. "The others, who organized the trip, picked the match-ups a long time ago. They put Mary Elizabeth in a different cabin from Noreen. I just went with the program."

"Why?" he said. "I mean why were Noreen and Mary Elizabeth to be in different cabins?"

"Look, I didn't lay out the details of this fiasco." Esbeth detected a bit of edge in her own voice but couldn't do anything about it. "Nor did I expect Noreen to be dead because of it."

Baxter cleared his throat. Esbeth suspected it was to give her a chance to rein in her emotions. "One or two of the other women tell me you have something of a reputation back in Austin as an amateur detective, that you've helped solve a case or two. I hope"—he hesitated—"that you won't feel any pressing urge to pitch in and help here."

Esbeth stood up so abruptly that the chair beneath her slid backward with a screech across the wooden floor. Her face felt flushed. She looked around the room. Everyone seemed to be staring at her, though she knew they weren't—most were busy in little head-to-head conversations among themselves. When she looked back at Baxter, the friendly, approachable look was gone from his face, and the blued-steel look of a cop had taken its place.

He held up a stiff forefinger, never said a word. He just pointed back down at the chair.

When she was just a hair calmer, she bent toward him and said in a low, steady voice, "A lot of times, I have to confess, I've ignored the law, gone my own way, and solved the case in spite of them, bowled them over a time or two. But this time, I don't *want* to be involved in finding Noreen's murderer. I just want the job done quickly."

He stared up at Esbeth. "I can't think of any reason, at least this early," he said, "why you might be lying to me."

Esbeth blinked, looked around, and saw the knotty pine walls, the mounted fish, and other trophies along the wall. Then she got her bearings, looked down, found the chair, pulled it back under her, and sat down across from him at the table again.

He said, "We're going to get along a lot better if you just provide good, level information with me."

"I want you to be aware that anything I might have said that would have pointed at a motive ought to be taken lightly at this point."

"You're way, way ahead of me," he wedged in, his face locked with hers. "I'm not shopping for anything so refined as a confession. I'm still getting a preliminary feel for the players here." He spoke softly, in a calming tone. But bedrock and cold steel were in his words.

"I guess I overreacted about Mary Elizabeth, huh? It's just that... if she were here... well, she'd be my first pick as a suspect. I'm really more than half-glad she isn't here."

"She's...?"

"In Austin. I just got off the phone talking with her. I'm the one taking her place on the trip, remember?"

"We established that. Why *didn't* she come?"

"Instead of me?"

"Instead of you."

"Well," Esbeth said, "for one, she's a lady my age and just broke her hip barely a week ago."

He nodded. Earlier, he had a tendency to let out small puffs of breath when she was rattling his chain. Now he just stared into her with those piercing pale blue eyes, and Esbeth had to say she squirmed a bit.

"Anything else you'd like to add?" he said.

"Nope."

Esbeth got up and went back to mingle with the others while Sheriff Baxter questioned the rest of those waiting. She had barely sat down in front of a cup of coffee when Garlena came rushing over to her. "I'm so glad you're along, Esbeth. I know at least you'll be able to do something about this."

Esbeth's head rocked up from the steaming cup, and she snapped at her, "Why does everyone always figure me for the one to fix things? All I want right now is to be alone a while, to let someone else wrap all this up." Before she knew it, she had risen to her feet and was stomping out of there. She didn't know what was behind it, except that being an amateur P.I. wasn't fun just then. She felt sick. She felt guilty. Esbeth swore to herself that no matter what, she would have nothing to do with the case.

In spite of all that, as she walked back to her cabin later in the damp and dark evening, she found herself thinking most about the spatters of blood she had seen on Bo Emma's shoes.

"Where in blue blazes have you been?" The room was solid black all around Esbeth, as dark as the night outside through the open door behind her.

She recognized Abby's voice. Abby struck a match and moved across to the kerosene lamp. As the lamp's light grew, the room took a shape. Abby sat at the table, where she had been waiting in the dark. The door banged closed behind Esbeth. Besides the lantern, there was only the dim red glow from the Franklin stove. It wasn't much of a glow, and the room was on the cool side. Abby had a blanket wrapped around her shoulders.

"Man alive," she said, "it was 'bout dark enough in here I was gonna have to light a second match to see if the first one was lit."

Esbeth must have grunted a response as she dragged her tired frame across the room and lowered herself into a chair at the table. Knowing that a killer was still on the loose made her kind of skittish. Coming in to find Abby waiting in the dark hadn't been all that great for her nerves. She hadn't seen her leave the dining area, yet she'd made it back to the cabin before Esbeth.

"Where've you been?" Abby repeated. The light from the lamp gave her skin a ghostly greenish-yellow tinge. Strange shadows played across her face, emphasizing her prim tendency to press her lips tightly together.

"I had to call Mary Elizabeth again. I promised to let her know how everything went."

"Did you wake her up?"

"No," Esbeth said. "It's a couple hours different in Austin. Remember?"

"How did she react to hearing 'bout Noreen? I'll bet she hasn't had so much fun since the legs fell off her hamster."

"She didn't sound all that glad," Esbeth said. "She hoped they catch whoever did it."

"And when they do," Abby said between clenched teeth, "I hope they rip off the head and tear off the limbs and shove the dripping stubs down the neck hole."

Of all of them, Abby was the biggest churchgoer and Bible quoter. But as Noreen had once said in describing Abby, "There's a darker side to everyone, and if you find a mob with torches and tongs out to do in the unrighteous, she'll not only be in it but may be at the head of it."

"I really do think the news hit Mary Elizabeth kind of hard," Esbeth said.

"Oh, come on, Esbeth." Abby leaned back in her chair. The kerosene lamp light lit only part of her—kind of spooky, actually. "You know and I know that if she was here, we'd know who killed Noreen."

"Well, she's all the way in Austin," Esbeth said.

"So she says. But you know that woman can lie like a congressman."

Esbeth struggled for a while as to what to say. She knew it was late but didn't even want to raise her arm to look at her watch. She finally managed, "I'm still so shook up about all this I probably rattle like a maraca."

"You are gonna investigate, ain't ya?"

"If I was, I'd start with Bo Emma's shoes."

"What about them?"

"The red stains on them."

"Oh, those." Abby let out a puff of breath. "Those stains were red yesterday, and they'll be red tomorrow too. They're raspberry stains. Blood turns brown as it dries. You're the one who told me that. Don't you recall?"

"I wish that I could give a good never mind right now. I'm so stark tired to the bone."

"Esbeth Walters. This is so unlike you. You've always been our avenging angel, and now when we really need you."

"I'm just not up to it."

"And cranky besides."

"I hope you all didn't invite me here expecting me to be Miss Congeniality.

Abby said, "Now don't you rare back and have a hissy fit. You know darn well we asked you when Mary Elizabeth flared up, and Lord knows the heart of that business floated over the dam years ago."

"You just said it," Esbeth offered. "Any real motive Mary Elizabeth had is long ago stale. That was when Jimmy broke off with her and married Noreen. All of us are over that now, even Mary Elizabeth. Even that mess about Bert Carson isn't enough. Besides, the killer has to be someone here. It's all too much of a tangle for me, or anyone."

"Say what you like, Mary Elizabeth was planning to come on this trip, right up to the last moment. Then there was the business with Shanna and Bo Emma's divorce."

"What's that have to do with anything?"

"Why, honey, where have you been? Don't you know about all that? It sounds like there's lots about this you don't know."

"No, and I don't want to right now. I just want to close my eyes." Esbeth stood up, wobbled just the tiniest bit, and began to move toward her room.

"How very, very unlike you. It's hard to believe you're the same person who would've normally lit into this even if the law asked you not to, especially if they said not to. You'd push to find the killer no matter what the consequences, even if it harelipped every cow in Texas."

Esbeth said nothing.

That didn't stop Abby, who went on, "But if you're dead set on not doing the one thing you do best, well, it looks like I'll just have to pick up the threads myself."

She said a lot more. But Esbeth closed the door to her room behind her. Whatever else Abby had to say trailed off behind the thickness of the hewn log barrier. In seconds, as soon as she could peel the frame in the dark and climb into bed, Esbeth was headed into a deep and dreamless sleep.

Chapter 24: The Dark Side of Romance

Esbeth woke the next morning early, in that kind of mental fog in which she was hoping everything had been a dream, but it wasn't.

Her bed was covered by two thick homemade quilts. She pushed off the cozy covers and forced herself out and started to dress, even though the room was so cool she thought she might be able to see her breath. It was probably seventy or eighty degrees back in the Austin area. She sought to focus on that and enjoy the cool. But there was no fooling herself. She felt cool enough to snap like an icicle. Once she had dressed in her regular Maine outfit, including her Red Wing boots and a jacket this time, she slipped quietly from her bedroom through the small living area with the now-cool Franklin stove. The door to Abby's room was closed. Esbeth trod carefully so as not to wake her.

Outside the cabin, the cool morning air, still moist in the dim light, woke her the rest of the way. In the state of mind she'd been in the previous night, she had never paused to wonder where poor Shanna was going to sleep. Certainly not in the cabin where Noreen's body had been found. Esbeth supposed they'd found a spot for her—must have found one for Sheriff Baxter, too, she figured, since she could see his biplane tied up at the pier beside the boats on the lake that spread out along the camp. The lake looked calm and dark, disappearing into a haze of mist a hundred or so yards from the pier. Dimples from rising brook trout dappled the otherwise glassy-still surface. She knew of no roads to the lodge. You could only get up there by biplane or boat. They'd had to leave a rental car parked where the lodge boat had picked them up a few days ago.

The lights were on in the lodge dining room, which she hoped didn't mean they'd been on all night. She pushed through the door, and the warmth of the room embraced her. The smell of coffee and bacon in the background added to the room's coziness. Something baking wafted along in the background of the dominant smells. That was one of the lodge's claims to fame. Lamant's daughter, Phyllis, baked every day. She made muffins, biscuits, pies, and cakes. She had been married, had moved back when she got divorced. Esbeth had had a fleeting thought earlier that perhaps she had married just to get away from the maiden name of Phyllis Willis. But names aside, boy, could she cook. With that in mind, it was a wonder to look at Lamant and realize how thin he was. The specimen himself sat at his favorite corner table, pipe smoke curling up around him. He wasn't reading or anything, just sitting with a plain white porcelain coffee mug in front of him. He stared ahead at nothing, at least nothing Esbeth could see.

She poured herself a mug from the large chrome dispenser, ambled over, and sat across from Lamant to be sociable. He stared awhile before he noticed her. When he did see her, he just nodded.

"My, it does get cool up here in the mornings," she said.

He nodded slowly. A puff of smoke put a period on the nod.

"Have you lived up here long?" she asked.

His eyes had drifted from her. They swung back. They didn't look pained, but it seemed clear that conversation wasn't a craving with him. He finally answered. "Yep."

"Just how long *have* you lived up here?"

Another wincing look. "'Bout forty year."

"My." Esbeth thought of the winters, when she'd heard it could get fifty below zero. "Doesn't the weather ever get to you?"

She might have detected a touch of anger in his eyes this time. Perhaps he was one of those people who had to charge their batteries by being alone. She could relate to that. After a pause, he said, "Well, 'bout three month a year, it gets hotter'n the devil 'round here."

His attention swung almost immediately to a fixed spot on the far wall. Esbeth looked that way, and there wasn't so much as a stuffed fish there to hold his attention. She eased up and went over to the wall map of the lodge area. She had her boots on and might as well use them. She swallowed the last of the coffee in her cup, figured she'd do breakfast justice later. Esbeth hated to interrupt Lamant once again from whatever he was studying so hard, but she said, "There are two trails that go down to the river where the landlocked salmon are supposed to spawn. Does it matter which of them I take?"

"Not to me it don't," he said.

Well, that was all of that she needed of an early morning. She put down her mug and headed for the out of doors.

As soon as the door had closed behind her, a voice called out from the back kitchen stoop. "Aren't you another early one?"

There stood Phyllis, daughter of motormouth Lamant. She was bundled and coming in from carrying out some scraps to the dump out at the edge of the woods just short of the blueberry fields. From her looks, she was another argument for opposites—while Lamant was of the Jack Spratt variety, she was not. She was a stocky blond woman with a cushiony build and not only smiled often but chatted whenever they met.

"It's not jeezly cold yet, but you southern women oughtta have a care you don't catch a chill," she cautioned.

Esbeth zipped her jacket closed. "I'll be careful. Thanks." She started off along one of the trails.

"Later," Phyllis called after her.

Esbeth followed the path, felt the forest floor crunching with each step, smelled the cool damp mustiness of the woods, saw steam rising slowly from the ground where it was warmer than the air. Where the path didn't carve a brown line along the floor of the woods, all of the space around her was filled with ferns and moss-covered logs. Most of the trees that rose around her had bark that was wet and black. It all seemed ever so much cooler than the furnace she'd left back in Texas. She tried again to cheer herself by the pleasant change, found herself staring down at the dirt, twigs, and scattered leaves of the trail. It felt cool in the woods, perhaps getting cooler as she neared the river. It woke her up, shook her out of what seemed a long sleep.

The path got wider as she neared the sound of roaring water. Steam rose in clouds from the river. It formed a thick layer of mist that covered the river, made the far bank impossible to see. As she got closer, she could see through the lower level of the mist, could make out water tumbling in white fury, with only a few slick spots behind protruding rocks. The slicks were dimpled by hatching bugs, occasionally marked by the splash of some fish rising to feed—some landlocked salmon, or one of the brookies, or some lone big brown trout. Esbeth breathed the cool air, felt very much revived. Then she looked down and saw a bundle of cloth at the stream's edge.

She recoiled then forced herself to edge closer. On the way, she grabbed at a long, forked dead limb that lay along the bank, used it to push at the cloth in the river. It resisted at first, gave a sudden roll at last, and bobbed back to the surface. From the bundle of clothing, a face washed pale and startled stared straight up at nothing. She heard a startled scream, realized it came from herself. The face belonged to Abby.

T he next few hours were ones Esbeth would long recall as among the busiest, most emotionally stressed, and least productive of her antique life. At the time, everything was such a blur that she would be surprised if she remembered a thing.

Biplanes were landing every hour. A helicopter settled down in the small green plot that passed for a lawn. New boats pulled up to the pier, many bearing the same official Aroostook County shield as on the newly arrived planes, though one plane had a state seal—the state medical examiner had finally arrived.

Sheriff Baxter, she understood, had been in his plane and heading back toward Caribou to handle some of the regular county sheriff business when he'd gotten a radio call from one of the two deputies he'd left behind. He'd had to turn back when he learned another body had been found. Esbeth had heard mention of this being the biggest county east of the Mississippi more than a couple of times. She guessed that was to let them know how thin he was being spread. But it wasn't like he would be called over to help out in metropolitan Presque Isle or anything. They had their own police department there. In fairness to Baxter, the country did spread from New Brunswick to the east all the way to Quebec province to the west.

If she had been Baxter, she might have felt crowded by the incoming expertise, the ME coming in and all. But he seemed to be rolling well with it all. Lamant Willis, when he wasn't just missing, appeared to be going to pieces in small chunks. Not that he became talkative or anything, but rather he kept trying to turn what profit he could from the situation. He was nipped briefly in the bud when he tried to charge the newly arriving investigators for docking their planes and boats at his pier. One of the deputies pulled him aside for a few moments, may have said something about obstructing justice. Lamant didn't say anything back, nor was it possible to tell from his perpetual frown how he felt. But Esbeth did notice that his gas prices jumped, and the lodge seemed to be doing a land-office business in the extra pies and other pastries Phyllis was baking.

Esbeth sat at one of the tables with Shanna and Garlena. Bo Emma had dissolved in tears only a moment or two before. The rest of them didn't look like they feel much better. She knew she felt a healthy nagging gnaw of guilt for letting Abby try to pick up her slack.

"They say that travel is broadening," Garlena finally said, breaking a long silence at the table. "And I don't just mean the way Bo Emma's been eating. You stay all your life in Austin, and you never hear about so much as a mugging, and then you go on one trip... and boom."

Shanna and Esbeth agreed without having to speak. There wasn't much they could say to underscore that.

A shadow fell across their table. Baxter stood above them looking down at them as if any one of them might just top the suspect list, which Esbeth had to suppose was true.

"You ladies have a moment?"

"Time is all we have," Garlena snapped. "I hear that none of us can leave until all this gets cleared up."

"A usual precaution. Let's hope we get as quick a wrap as we can for everyone's sake."

"Won't matter much to Noreen nor Abby," Garlena said. "They're as graveyard dead as you can get." Her jaw clicked shut with the finality only an older person could manage.

"You mind?" Baxter asked, glancing at each of them. He slid a chair back and sat down at their table.

He looked directly across the table at Esbeth. "Spoke with your sheriff down there in Travis County," he said. "He said to tell you that any time you could pass by his office he'd appreciate it." He cocked his head, waited for a reply from her that wasn't forthcoming. "Pass by, not stop in," Baxter said, pressing it. When Esbeth still didn't answer, he asked, "Okay, which of you would like to tell about Noreen and Mary Elizabeth again, and what brings you all up here?"

None of them leaped at the opportunity. So he looked at Esbeth again and said, "You *do* all know each other, don't you?"

Esbeth sighed then said, "Garlena, Noreen, Abby, and myself were all in school together."

"High school?"

"In those days, it was every grade. Not everyone finished back then, and of those who did, not many are left."

"Fewer now," he said.

"Fewer now," she echoed. She gave that a moment to steep then continued. "We were all as thick as thieves back then, until recently."

He waited, a look of stone-carved patience etched in the weathered wrinkles of his face. Garlena looked away. Shanna bent closer and was listening hard.

"Jimmy Dolan," Esbeth said. "He was the catch of our class. I suppose every school has one. Mary Elizabeth and he went steady all through school, but in the end, he married Noreen."

"How does that have to do with this?"

"The rest of us were bridesmaids at the wedding. I was maid of honor. Mary Elizabeth was asked to be one of the bridesmaids but declined."

"That was a long, long time ago."

"Before you were born, I'm afraid," Esbeth said.

"So Mary Elizabeth never married."

"Well, she did, finally, to someone from the same class who had dropped out of school to work." That was common then. Her brother had done the same thing—dropped out, that was.

"She settled," Baxter said. "But how did that affect things?"

"That husband disappeared on Mary Elizabeth, went away to get work, and never came back that we knew of." Esbeth sighed. "Sure, there was a lot of tension there for a long time, but anything over fifty years old gets a bit silly or petty. Only recently, Mary Elizabeth and Noreen finally buried the hatchet."

"Right after we buried Jimmy Dolan," Garlena inserted.

A new furrow started to show on Baxter's forehead. Or, at the least, one of his regular furrows was more noticeable. "Every race or contest," he said, "has a runner-up, I guess."

"Well, that doesn't have to be how you look at it." Shanna exploded out of her chair and stood wide-eyed down at them. In the general hubbub of the dining area right then, it made almost no waves. Shanna stopped mid-sentence, blinked a couple of times, and sat back down. "Sorry," she said. She looked around at them as if expecting them to go on, as if they could after that.

"You've known all these ladies quite a while," Baxter said to Esbeth, drawing attention away from Shanna but giving her the corner of his eye.

Shanna's face still held a tint of red. Hers was normally a very long pale face. Her black hair had a front clump that was a premature fluff of white, which she allowed to spray out in a fluffy burst. The rest of her raven-wing-black hair was dyed, they suspected, and drawn back into a severe ponytail.

"You don't think any of that had anything to do with what's happened up here, do you?" He asked it of Esbeth, but he looked around at the others.

"I haven't the foggiest," Garlena said. Esbeth was glad to have her do the talking. "You always think people are going to act differently when they get older—you know, calmer, more mellow. But what I've noticed is that, if anything, some emotions get even more intense with the years of stewing. You know, the old jealousy and hate, love and all that."

"A lot of repressed stuff eventually does boil over the pot," Baxter agreed. He turned to Esbeth and asked, "You speak with your friend Mary Elizabeth yet?"

"I called her a couple of times. Once right after what happened to Noreen."

"If you folks'll excuse me," Shanna said, "I'll go check on Bo Emma." She had her calm voice and normal color back now. To Baxter, she said, "If you're going to be busy here a while, maybe I'll take a long soak."

"Fine with me," Baxter said.

As soon as Shanna was out of sight and hearing, Garlena asked Baxter, "Is she your roomie?"

"Well, until we clear the crime scene area in the other cabin. There are separate bedrooms, after all. All the other cabins were occupied. Two of my deputies took one cabin. It seemed better that I take the spare room in Shanna's cabin."

"Probably the most intimate she's been with a man in years," Garlena said. "Except for that one flurry way back when."

"She single?" Baxter asked.

"Like me," Esbeth said. "Never married."

"Any story there?" Baxter asked.

"Not about me." Esbeth looked at Garlena. Her white hair was straight but not as long as Shanna's hair.

Garlena sighed. "She was keen on a fellow, Mason, who married Bo Emma."

"And?"

"Bo Emma just divorced him not too long back. But Shanna didn't pursue him once he was free. Now the two of them, Shanna and Bo Emma, are pals again. The boy, if you want to call him that, was Mary Elizabeth's grandson."

"This is more tangled than I thought." Baxter took no notes. But Esbeth suspected he forgot little. He gave her his full attention again, "I imagine you got a pretty cool reception from the law when you helped solve cases in the past."

"You can say that with bells on," Garlena answered for Esbeth.

"I'd like to ask you a favor." Esbeth could tell this wasn't sitting all that well with him. He paused for a moment before he got the rest of it out. "I'd like to take back what I said earlier and ask for your help on this. Even with all the new faces here, I'm short on help, and you know some of the players. And..." He stretched it out, sighed before going on. "Your Sheriff Danvers, in addition to everything else he said, did say that you were one top-notch detective, that you'd actually solved some cases that might have left him stumped. I'd be glad for that kind of help right now if it means I can wrap this up quickly."

"I'm not one of the suspects?"

"Of course you are. But that doesn't change anything. All of you are." He gave Garlena a glance. "But let's put that aside. What do *you* think happened?"

Esbeth hesitated, looked at Garlena. If Esbeth hadn't been ready by then to pitch in anyway, the twinge of guilt she still felt would have nudged her in. "Abby was up by the waterfall, beneath the falls, not at the top. She was pushed or fell into the river, drowned before she was swept up to the bank where I found her."

"You didn't go upstream and look around, did you?" Baxter squinted. Around them in the room, men were still scurrying about. There was nothing like the hustle of uniformed men to make a place seem like a war zone. It gave the place a faint patriotic stir.

"No. I didn't want to mess up any footprints or anything."

"How are you able to picture how it happened, then?"

"She wasn't at the top of the falls, or she would probably have been banged up more. With the current as strong as it was, I have to think that she would have been farther downstream if she'd gone in where I found her."

"Time of death?"

"The water was cold enough it probably makes determining her time of death hard, but she *had* been in the water a while."

"Pretty good as it goes," he said. "There were signs of a struggle farther upstream, but..." He caught some glitter of interest in Esbeth's eyes. "That's all we have. Hers were the only prints going to the falls."

"Then who did she struggle with?" Garlena asked.

"Now that," Baxter said, "is a very good question."

They sat and mulled over that for a few moments, the din of the other officers' chatter bouncing off the knotty pine walls. Baxter swung his glance back and forth between Garlena and Esbeth. "Why does each of you think of Mary Elizabeth when the topic of motive comes up? You said she had reconciled with Noreen."

Garlena glanced at Esbeth, who shrugged. Garlena said, "There was a new wrinkle in the old tale."

He looked at her.

"A man," she said.

"One who had been hanging around Mary Elizabeth," Esbeth said. His eyes swung back to her like he was watching a tennis match.

"But he switched his attention to Noreen when Noreen's husband died," Garlena filled in.

"Ow," Baxter said. "I didn't know that so much romance went on with..." His voice trailed off.

"We're old," Garlena snapped, "but our feelings haven't been removed. Yeah, we still have romances, just like real people. The urge just has more to do with companionship now than with the old slap and tickle."

"Okay," Baxter said. "I was off base there. So Noreen ended up with the man a second time. I see. I'll bet Mary Elizabeth didn't like that."

"That," said Garlena, "is putting it mildly."

Despite the hubbub of all the added lawmen hanging around and hogging the dining area as well as the phone on Willis's office desk, Esbeth finally was able to squeeze in a call later in the afternoon. She was reluctant to call Alex or Scott. The two of them had been wrestling around, she thought, in the awkward early stages of their own romance back in Austin. Where once she had been friends with both of them, now they seemed to spend most of their time together, had been too busy for Esbeth. She had begun to stay in her house a little too much, not trapped but restless, yet at the same time not eager to go out. At first, she thought she just needed a rest from people. Then she realized she was withdrawing. She guessed people did that sometimes, though it wasn't something she made a habit of doing.

The phone back in Austin was ringing, but no one picked it up right away back there. Part of Esbeth wanted to just go to her cabin and lie down, enjoy the cool of the evening creeping in, think of Noreen and Abby's deaths, and maybe nurse some sadness at her own mortality. But she was a doer and had to admit to that as well.

"Hello?" It was Alex's voice, answering at Scott's house.

"It's me," Esbeth said.

"Oh, Esbeth," Alex said, "I've been reading all about what happened to Noreen. You must feel awful."

Esbeth told her about Abby now, too, and heard her gasp.

"It makes everything here seem so petty," Alex said.

"Why, what's going on there? Are you two fighting?"

"Oh, just a bit," she admitted. "We were talking about our pasts..."

"Always a mistake," Esbeth said.

"And he was talking about his dead wife, made one of those Freudian slips, said something about fond mammaries."

"What he probably meant—"

"I know what he meant," she said.

"Maybe you shouldn't have been pumping him."

"Me? I never—"

"Who's swimming up de Nile now?" Esbeth asked. Before this turned into all-night dialogue, Esbeth asked, "Can you put Scott on?"

When he came on, Esbeth said, "Did you stop by and visit Mary Elizabeth like I asked?"

"Well, uh..."

"Well, uh, what?"

"I got her on the phone. But I got no answer at the house, haven't had a chance to check back. I've been bogged down with one thing and another."

"Oh, Scott."

"What?"

"I want you to try again, in person. If you don't get in to see her, I've got an errand I want you to run."

"And what'll you be doing while I run my legs off?" he asked.

"They're keeping us up here until this gets straightened out, one way or another," Esbeth said. She was thinking of Mason coming between Bo Emma and Shanna, the parallel between that and Mary Elizabeth and Noreen. Maybe there was nothing to it. But in a murder investigation, she hated anything even close to coincidence. It was worth looking into. "I guess I'll find some way to keep busy."

He said, "I imagine you will."

Chapter 25: Bear with Me

"What is it with you and Shanna?" Esbeth asked, pushing away a limb of a fir tree that grew out into the path. The thing about Maine that kept pounding in on her was how very green everything was, though she was sure it wasn't that way year-round.

"You mean you don't know?" Bo Emma said from where she was huffing along behind Esbeth, gradually lagging farther. She was far enough back that she didn't have to worry about getting swatted with any of the limbs Esbeth let go of as she pushed along the narrow brown pine-needle-and-dirt trail. The usual ferns lined the forest floor around them.

She just wanted to talk with her. It was one reason she had leaped at the opportunity to be alone with Bo Emma and away from the others when she suggested slipping away to the berry fields, though she doubted Baxter would have approved the outing. She didn't picture Bo Emma driven by a need for exercise. But all the extra folks at the lodge had eaten all of the pies, muffins, and blueberry pancakes—and *that* did seem to threaten her.

Esbeth stopped for a minute to give Bo Emma a rest. That was something when she thought about it, since Esbeth gave away a good forty years in the bargain. Bo Emma plodded up the trail and bent forward, grabbing her knees and puffing while she caught her breath. As Esbeth had said before, there was plenty of Bo Emma.

"You know," she huffed, "the only time I ever lost—*huff*—two—*huff*—hundred pounds?" She was barely able to speak again.

"No," Esbeth said, thinking hard, stretching to imagine. "When was that?"

"When I divorced Mason." She straightened, and her head rocked back when she laughed. It was a roly-poly cheerful laugh, and it was one reason Esbeth was glad to be around her right then.

Her chuckles slowed down, and she looked around for someplace to sit, a log or a stump. There was nothing but the wet dark bark of the tree trunks and the thick carpet of ferns that glowed chartreuse green in the light that filtered down through the high canopy tops of the trees. She didn't spot anything, so she eased slowly down onto the moist trail.

"You mind if I set just a spell? I'm plumb tuckered."

"Suit yourself," Esbeth said. "I'll just stand and rest if that's okay." She saw a salamander shoot across the ground beside Bo Emma's hip but didn't point it out, not knowing how she felt about such critters. Esbeth sure didn't want her to have some kind of heart attack and have to carry her out of these woods. They'd walked a good hour so far—not at a rocket pace, mind you, and they still had a piece to go.

"It was Mason come between us," she said looking up at Esbeth, her eyes halfway between hurt puppy and determined.

"I thought you two were having troubles anyhow? Wasn't that the reason for splitting up?"

"Oh, sure. Mason had been known to drink more than he could walk with. It's like they used to say about Daddy. 'Don't cut no fire-wood, 'cause Daddy's comin' home with a load.'"

"He thumped on you a bit, too, didn't he?"

"That goes with the program, I guess," she sighed. "It was the same with Daddy."

"It doesn't have to be," Esbeth said between clenched teeth, though she knew she shouldn't be surprised. But Bo Emma had hit a nerve. Esbeth really didn't care much for butting in and steering other people's lives, though it pained her to see some people accept things they didn't need to live with, especially abusive men. "Why'd you say Shanna figured in the divorce?"

"Did you know that I walked in on 'em, caught 'em together?"

"Were they... busy?"

"She was covering him like dew covers Dixie."

"What did you do?"

"I didn't do nothin', but Mason did. He jumped up and hit me so hard the back of my dress flew up like a window shade."

Esbeth tried to smile back at the chuckle she managed now, but it was a chore. "I understand you leaving your husband after that. I'm surprised you and Shanna ever reconciled."

"We'd always been best friends. And she never hurt me none, at least the way Mason done." Her face beamed up at Esbeth, open and honest, a rounded expanse of smooth pink skin and dimples. It was hard to believe she was capable of hate at all. "Sides," she said, "if you went through life choppin' everyone off at the knees whoever did you any little kind of accidental harm, well, you'd have no friends at all."

"Shanna and Mason being together was an accident?"

"You gotta realize how lonely she gets. She just hurts inside, or she'd have never said such nasty things to me."

"Nasty like what?"

"Oh, little stuff. Like when she said, 'on most people a double chin doesn't look as cute as it does on you.' Another time she said I'd just traded one lust for another—eating now. You know, kind of backhanded like, little stuff just to rock my boat. But I understood it all onced I saw how she was about Mason."

"But she didn't marry him once he split up with you."

"'Course not. Who would? The man was pond scum, like most of 'em are. An' I think the whole thing lost its charm after there was nothing to compete over. That's one a the things Shanna and I agree on now."

Esbeth shook her head. It was all one too many for her.

"I know what you're thinkin'," Bo Emma said as she started to struggle back to her feet. Esbeth reached out and pulled with all she had to help get Bo Emma upright. "Why take up with Mason in the first place? Well, I was pretty young when I started up with him. And you know what folks say. A young woman's love is like dew, just as apt to fall on a horse turd as on a rose."

Esbeth couldn't argue with that. They started off pushing their way along the trail again.

After a few more steps, Esbeth said, "I'm not too comfortable being so far from the lodge. Baxter told us to stay near."

"We ain't goin' nowhere," Bo Emma said. "It'd take a plane or boat to get us anywheres that would bother the good sheriff."

Esbeth wasn't so sure about that. But she was glad for the chance to get Bo Emma off to talk a bit, even though so far, she had done more huffing than talking. Lamant Willis had told them where to go, had given them the buckets. They'd hiked past the lodge's trash dump and had crossed the twin trails of a dirt road that Esbeth understood went all the way to Canada in either direction if your car's shocks were in great shape. They stayed on the small trail that after two or three more miles would stop at the edge of a deep-water trout lake. But they weren't going all the way to the lake. The woods around them began to thin, and in a few more steps Esbeth pushed through a couple of tight limbs and froze where she stood. All around them wide fields of rolling flat hills were covered by low, tightly packed bushes. There was a bluish tinge to the green of the bushes. Looking down low and in front of her, Esbeth could see the reason. Thick umbrella-shaped clumps of blueberries spread across the bushes around them. She'd never seen so many in her life, and here they stood in acres and acres of these bushes.

Bo Emma pushed out of the woods, looking damp and tuckered until she looked out across the fields Esbeth was staring at. "I've died and gone to blueberry heaven," she said.

Esbeth pulled the plastic buckets she carried apart and handed her one, keeping one for herself. "We'd best get picking. And remember, Bo Emma, don't eat any of the berries, especially those near the trail."

"Like someone was gonna come out here and poison us that way. I swear, Esbeth, you are plain paranoid."

"Just don't do it." Esbeth started picking.

"I got more control than you give me credit for," she muttered as she bent and started scooping up handfuls of blueberries, making sure Esbeth saw she dropped them in her bucket. "You think I got a tapeworm or something?"

"*There's* a perfect pet for you," Esbeth said. "A tapeworm. Goes where you go, eats what you eat."

Bo Emma shared a merry chuckle then said, "This cool air up here does give me an appetite, though."

"Well, save it until we get back and can wash off these berries."

"We wouldn't even have to be out here pickin' more," she grumped, "if them lawmen hadn't et up what Phyllis had picked 'fore we got here." But, like Esbeth, she bent to the task and started picking.

It wasn't all that hard. The berries were in such handy bunches, and the bushes had no thorns. The sky was clear and blue, but the sun wasn't making it too hot. A light breeze was blowing as well. Esbeth toyed with taking off the sweater she wore over her flannel shirt but decided not to just yet. It wouldn't take too long to fill their buckets, thick as the berries were. They could have filled dozens of buckets from as wide a field of blueberries as it was.

They stayed hard at it for an hour or so. It was the kind of work in which you kept your head down and focused on how fast the bucket was filling, gave yourself little pep talks about how quickly you'd be done. But every once in a while, you did have to stand upright and stretch a bit, unless you wanted to end up ringing bells at Notre Dame. It was in one of those stretches that Esbeth saw a black lump of coal in the field downwind from them a good hundred yards, but it was growing as it came their way. Bo Emma was staring that way too. She said, "Now what for land's sake do you suppose that is?"

"*Bear*!" Esbeth shouted to her.

Bo Emma's face turned to Esbeth, and the look on her face would be registered with Esbeth forever. It was a stark confession that she knew she wasn't going to be able to run as far and as fast as they needed to go. Then an embarrassed shift happened as she saw Esbeth, realized she was in her eighties and had pretty well put behind her the days of the checkered flag as far as distance running went.

"Bo Emma," Esbeth said, hoping to snap her from her trance. "Put down your bucket and start moving slowly and steadily toward the woods. But don't run just yet. Walk."

"But I can't leave you."

"Just go," Esbeth hissed.

Bo Emma put her bucket down and started a slow ambling gate, with just a touch of briskness to it. Watching the bear come rapidly closer, Esbeth thought Bo Emma's gait resembled that of the bear more than a bit. Esbeth gave her some lead time, but she was making slow going and was only half the distance to the woods. Esbeth put her bucket down, raised her arms high over her head, and waved her arms. The bear rose on its haunches, stopped for a moment, and stared at Esbeth. There was no question that by now it had fixed on her. She glanced over at Bo Emma and saw that she had paused to bend and huff a while. Damnation.

When Bo Emma first started to move Esbeth noticed that the bear's direction changed a bit. The bear veered her way, drawn by the movement—they were a bit like a cat that way, she'd heard. She waved her arms now until she was sure she had the bear's attention, then Esbeth took off at a trot deeper into the field, away from Bo Emma. The bear dropped to the ground and started to come after her, and she was sure it was going faster now than it had before.

Tell her a bear wasn't wily. She realized that it was cutting across the blueberry bushes at a slant, seeking to get ahead of her to cut her off. Well, that was good to the extent Esbeth took it farther from Bo Emma. She was running briskly along but realized that very soon the bear was going to beat her to the path ahead of her. Esbeth could see its red tongue hanging out as it bounded in its offbeat gallop across the bushes. She believed she imagined the flicker of its yellowed teeth, too, against the contrast of thick black fur, knew she could not see that yet.

When it was nearly at the path ahead of her, she stopped abruptly. Then she spun and started back along the path toward the woods. Maybe she had been running before, but for a seventy-year-old, she nearly flew now. She suspected that she could have seen Jesse Owens in her rearview mirror if he'd have been in the race. He wasn't, but the bear sure was. Esbeth could hear it crushing the bushes in the distance behind her. She was tired, plumb tuckered as Bo Emma said, but she ran on and never paused.

Ahead of her on the trail, still farther from the woods than she should have been, Esbeth could see Bo Emma. She had stopped to turn back and watch what Esbeth was doing, maybe hadn't caught on that Esbeth was trying to lure the bear away from her. "Run!" Esbeth tried to shout, but it came out as a hollow gasp.

Now that she saw that both Esbeth and the bear were coming in her direction, Bo Emma did finally turn and start moving toward the woods again. It was funny what you thought of as you were trotting along at Esbeth's age with a bear on your heels, but she knew she wasn't going to keep up this pace long, was probably already on borrowed jogging time. Her mind raced through any diversion she could think of, and her hands went down to her sides and felt the foil packages in the sweater pockets, the packages of complimentary peanuts she'd been given on the plane. As she ran, or slogged along by now, she tore one package open and rolled the peanuts in her palms until they were as ground as she could make them while on the run. Then she tossed the handful of peanuts and dust up behind her to settle back on the trail.

A few steps farther, she risked a head-turn back and saw that the bear slowed then stopped to nose around at the trail where the peanuts had fallen. He may have licked and sniffed a bit. Esbeth shifted her focus back to the trail and gained some space, even at the slowed pace she now moved. Her feet were still going, but her lungs weren't keeping up. A bear was a good motivator, but she really couldn't recommend running at her age.

When Esbeth sneaked another peek behind her, the bear was coming after her again, and she forced herself to keep moving while she tore the other pack of peanuts open. She'd heard bears liked peanuts, but this one must have found the last sample only a teaser. Bo Emma was barely moving and still not in the woods. Then she stopped to rest again. Esbeth was gaining on her, was going to be up to her soon. She tossed the last batch of peanuts and dust behind her and raced on, didn't even dare glance back that time.

She tried to shout but could barely squeak by the time she got up within Bo Emma's hearing. Between her own huffing, she called to Bo Emma to lie down and play dead. It was the only thing she could think of. She'd heard that bears wouldn't mess with you if they thought you were dead. But to Esbeth, the catch seemed to be that maybe that wouldn't work if they'd just been chasing you.

Esbeth's senses were a little overwhelmed right then, but she believed she could hear the bear coming at them. She knew she could probably overtake Bo Emma, even as slow as she was going herself. Then Bo Emma gave up on the running and lay down on the trail, too pooped probably to run any more. Esbeth didn't want to run past her. She stopped where she was and dropped to the slim dirt path herself. Her breathing wouldn't slow, as much as she tried to make it. She covered her head with her arms, hands tucked in under her sweater sleeves, and waited.

The plunging ambling thick steps that had been coming up the trail behind her slowed. Esbeth panted, her face pressed to the ground. Above her raspy breathing, she could hear slow steps coming toward her, thick fur scraping against the narrow bushes of the trail. Then she could hear the panting breath and hard sniffing of the bear. She either imagined or felt the bear's footpads along the path then felt something nudge her shoulder, a paw or nose. She could smell the bear now, a musky combination of not-too-clean thick fur and hot animal breath.

Her mind was playing terrible tricks on her, urging her to jump up and run, to scream, to relive her past. She forced herself to lie as still as she could. She wasn't one much for prayer, but the thought more than passed her mind as she lay there trembling inside and just waiting.

Esbeth tottered and wove out of the trail from the woods at last and could see the figures on the long wooden porch of the lodge. Light was failing, but she saw one of the two talking men make her out and shout or wave. Then a figure leaped off the porch and came running. As he got closer, she could make out that it was Sheriff Baxter.

"Bear," Esbeth gasped and staggered on. "Blueberry fields."

He got up to her and put an arm around her, led her toward the porch. "You crazy old ladies didn't go out to that, did you?" He stopped himself, called over to the porch. "Lamant, give me a hand here."

Willis stood stiff on the porch. He stared at Esbeth then shook himself and came over to help lead her up on the porch. They took her inside and set her down at one of the tables.

"Do you want anything?" Baxter said.

"Coffee," she said. Then, "Bo Emma, you've got to go bring her back."

"Just take it easy," Baxter said. "Get your breath back." He looked around inside the dining area. Shanna shot up from the table where she was sitting and rushed toward Esbeth. "Phyllis!" Baxter yelled.

"Oh, Esbeth," Shanna cried out to her, with none of her usual husky hauteur. "Someone get brandy," she shouted off behind her. She pushed Lamant Willis to one side and plopped into the chair next to Esbeth's, put an arm around her shoulders, and brought her face close to Esbeth's. "Tell me Bo Emma's okay. Please. Oh, Esbeth, please!"

Esbeth said, "She's back there."

"Do we need to send a group out there?" Baxter leaned closer from the other side of the table, his words crisp and business-like. His eyes were intense and drilling through Esbeth, then his head snapped to the other dining-room dwellers who were crowding around. He yelled, "Give her room, everyone. Let her breathe." He swung back to her. "What possessed the two of you to go to those fields? Bears hang around the trash dump year-round. They get positively possessive when the fields are full of blueberries."

It was hard to see all the faces that loomed closer, pulled back again. Esbeth wanted to see the expression on every face.

"Hey, she's all right!" a voice shouted, riding over all the other chatter in the room. It came from near the door.

"We know," Shanna said. "She's right here."

"I mean Bo Emma." Garlena's shout this time brought the small dining room crowd to a pin-clattering quiet. Her words were flat and held no sparkle or humor.

She plowed through the circle of people and bent over the checkered cloth, her gaze locked with Shanna's, not Esbeth's.

"I just saw Bo Emma sneaking in, trying to get to her cabin without any of us seeing her."

"Why in the ever-loving world would she do that?"

Garlena leaned closer to Shanna. "Don't you see? It's one of Esbeth's little detective ruses. Bo Emma says someone might've set them up to be attacked by a bear. Esbeth here, it seems, was hoping to see if one of us acted guilty or something."

"Which you pretty much spoiled," Esbeth admitted.

Baxter's eyes were open wide with shock and just a tiny touch of admiration.

"Oh, Esbeth, how could you?" Shanna's face flushed scarlet. She jumped up from the table and pushed backward into and past the people crowded behind her. Once through, she spun and ran for the door.

Garlena leaned closer until her face was within inches of Esbeth's.

"You, Esbeth Walters, are dumber than a box of hair if you think either one of us had anything to do with Noreen or Abby's deaths; and we sure as muddled porridge didn't send you anyplace where the likes of you and Bo Emma could run footraces with a bear."

She spun on a heel and stomped dramatically out of the room.

Baxter stood staring at Esbeth for a moment then said, "You had Shanna figured for it, didn't you?"

Esbeth gave what could be taken as a nod or a head shake and continued to look around at the faces of the small crowd.

Lamant Willis snorted through his nose and turned away. Phyllis shook her head, gave Esbeth a sad and disappointed smile, then headed back for the kitchen. One by one, the others who had been in the dining area left or moved away.

When it was finally just the two of them—Baxter with a bemused look on his face while she appeared less confused—he looked over her smudged and torn outfit and ended by staring at her face.

"This plan of yours," he said, "no doubt looked better on the drawing board than it does now."

Still wrinkled, in spirit as well as appearance, Esbeth made her way over to the phone before heading to her cabin for a much-needed cleaning.

"So, how goes it there in the frosty north?" Scott said when he picked up and she'd identified herself.

"A mite frosty right now," she said. "You get to visit with Mary Elizabeth?"

"Well, not exactly."

"Just the phone, huh?"

"Look, I gave it a shot."

"I need a favor. I need you to run that errand I mentioned earlier," Esbeth said. "Then I need you to come up here as soon as you can."

"No 'please'?"

"Please," she said.

"What's the matter?" he said. "Won't your friends up there play with you anymore?"

"As a matter of fact," she said, "no."

It was very late afternoon, almost early evening, when their boat finally pulled up to the dock. It bobbed in the waves of the small wake it had made. Esbeth stood waiting along the path up to the lodge. Scott and Alex came walking up the trail, Scott carrying his small duffle and Alex's bigger Hartman suitcase.

"You're sure looking fit," Scott said as soon as he was within hearing. "These northern woods must agree with you. Getting lots of exercise?"

Esbeth let a hard snort of air snap through her nostrils but otherwise didn't respond to that.

"Didn't take you all that long to alienate yourself in yet another state," Scott said. He was looking around at the line of hewn-log cabins that circled the lake with the lodge at their center.

Alex gave him a brief look, one Esbeth couldn't read. But when he caught it, it made him suddenly quiet.

"Did you bring it?" Esbeth asked Scott.

"And paid the price getting it, too, I might add," Scott said. "Had to put up with Dirty-Fingernail Huff's breath and then deal with all those weird animals he has in the country place of his. A raccoon bit me."

"She only scratched you with her little fingernail," Alex said. To Esbeth, she confided, "Probably sensed his latent masculine hostility."

"Latent?" Scott said. "I'd have drop-kicked the fur ball across the room if she hadn't shot away, and Huff got in the way."

"I hope you didn't alienate Huff," Esbeth said. "He's helped me a lot in the past."

"A man whose breath can melt a camera lens can't be alienated, Esbeth. And listen to who's talking."

"Right," Esbeth admitted. "I am low on allies here at the moment. Well, we'd better get you two settled if we're going to get an early start. It's a bit crowded. The sheriff and a few of his men are still around."

"I'll stay with you," Alex got out rather quickly, "You have a spare room, don't you?"

Esbeth glanced at Scott, who was looking out across the lake.

"He's a big boy," Alex said. "He can take care of himself."

What with one thing and another, including a long talk with Sheriff Baxter, Esbeth didn't get back to the cabin until just as the generator was being shut down for the night. But Alex had a couple of kerosene lanterns already lit, and the inside of the cabin was glowing as Esbeth crunched up the walk.

As Esbeth came through the door, Alex turned from where she was throwing a couple more pieces of wood into the Franklin stove. "What are you up to?" she asked. "You've been out there wandering around like the ghost of Hamlet's father for the better part of the evening."

"Just getting some last-minute details together," Esbeth said. "What, on another hand, is up with you and Scott?"

"Up? What do you mean?" Her mouth turned up at one corner in mock innocence.

When Esbeth didn't answer right away as she walked over and plopped into one of the straight-back chairs at the table, Alex said, "You were thinking the two of us were headed toward a romance, weren't you?"

"You're not?" The two of them hadn't started to act friendly until a year after Scott's wife had passed away.

"For a detective, I have to think that as far as crimes of the heart go, we've found your weak spot. Of course we're not. We've decided to be friends, just like you and Scott are."

"You're not an item?"

"You were jealous, weren't you? That's why you've been acting so odd."

"Me, odd?" Esbeth said.

"Oh, you old soft-hearted coot, you. You must have known how it would go with us. Really, though, Scott's a rare find. Don't you remember? You're the one who gave me a first glimpse of his real qualities. You said that some women think men only act truly nice when they want something. We agreed on that. But you said Scott was different from the rest, and you were right. A lifetime as a journalist has made him a world-class listener. What he needs most is someone to listen to, a connection. That, in my experience, is rare—kind of like finding a dance partner who'll let you lead. Sure, he's got a few burrs, but I'm just the file for them. You know what they say at the gym—no pain, no pain. But a romance? Aw, come on, Esbeth!"

Esbeth could hear noises of night settling in across Maine outside. Inside, it was cozy with the fire going and the crackle of the logs as a backdrop. But it felt good, very good to be talking.

"What is it?" Alex asked after a moment, reading something in Esbeth's face.

"I'm glad I called you two," Esbeth said at last. "I wasn't sure at first why I had. I guess Scott could have sent along what I asked him to fetch. But it's good to see the two of you."

"I think the two of us might have taken you for granted just a bit," Alex confessed. "We think of you as being tough…"

"As last year's taffy. I know. I guess I foster a bit of that. But I'll tell you the plain truth. Some people get houses and spend every ounce of free time caring for the lawn or some such; others get a car and wear the paint off washing and waxing it. But to me, my friends are the chief pride and labor of my life. You can't imagine how it is to lose a couple of life-long friends, ones I went to school with, back when we were small enough to be cutting paper clothes out of the Sears catalog for our cardboard dolls." Esbeth stopped, had a little froglet in her throat or something. After she'd cleared her throat, she told Alex, "Don't you go telling anyone back in Austin I'm not hard as a horned toad, though." But the rasp in her voice took any edge off that.

Alex nodded, rose, and headed toward her room. "Yeah. We'd better turn in. From the sounds of it, we have a full day. But at least all this should be over soon."

"I hope so," Esbeth agreed, "unless something breaks or comes untwisted."

Chapter 26: The Other Shoe Drops

For the first forty minutes of the ride early the next a.m., they bounced up two dirt ruts that passed as a road to the north leading toward the lodge's trash dump and then the blueberry fields. Baxter drove the jeep he'd commandeered from Lamant after stationing Alex and one of the remaining investigators at the phone. He glanced at his watch every few minutes.

They came to a crossroad at last, the one Bo Emma and Esbeth had had to cross before the trail narrowed to a single dirt path. "Right or left?" Baxter asked.

"Left, probably," Esbeth said.

He looked at her. Scott sat in the back seat, as usual saying very little. Ben Erickson, Baxter's chief deputy, sat in the back seat beside Scott. Ben wore a labored, patient look. As they were climbing into the jeep, Esbeth had heard him sigh to Baxter, "Whatever it takes."

"If we're wrong, we can always backtrack and try to make up time," Esbeth said. "But I think Abby knew something. If someone could walk across the dam, they'd..."

"What?" Baxter said.

"Be real close to the lodge, wouldn't they." Esbeth was looking along the road for any signs of wear, but it was hard to make out if a car had come through here. Trucks went by just often enough to keep the bushes and growth trimmed back. She couldn't make out any fresh signs a car might have made.

"What roads exist this far up are private ones," Ben explained to Scott. "Someone could get out here this way, but it's not easy, and that person would have to have a permit and pay to use the roads. That's why almost everyone comes by boat or plane. If anyone came from either direction, there would be a record of them at least."

"*That's* not our worry," Esbeth said. Then she added, "It's almost time."

"How's this look?" Baxter stopped the jeep.

Scott had the gadget Dirty-Fingernails Huff had sent along. He took it with him when he and Ben got out of the jeep. Scott turned it on, fiddled with the knobs a bit. He'd shown Esbeth how it worked earlier, how the little directional lights could hone in on and pinpoint a frequency. That part was up to him now.

Baxter leaned with both forearms across the steering wheel. He looked around them. While Scott and Ben muttered over the gadget Baxter watched the second hand on his wristwatch. "Now," he said. To Esbeth, he said quietly, "Do you think much about what drives people to murder?"

"More and more," Esbeth said. She wanted to say that it used to be hard to imagine but that she'd seen so much of it in the past few years that she'd become jaded, less surprised. But she was done talking.

After a few moments, an excited whisper came from Scott. "We're getting something. Back there." He pointed back along the road they'd come.

He and Ben hopped into the jeep. Baxter started it up, turned them around, and began to drive at a steady pace back along the road. Esbeth watched the screen on the face of the gadget Scott held. A red dot and sweeping lines flickered on the small black screen. "Here," Scott said.

Baxter stopped the jeep, let the motor run. He and Ben hopped out, went to the right side of the road, and leaned over a fallen tree that lay beside the road. They both bent and pulled. It came away easily, and a small road was visible now. The two of them sprinted back to the jeep. Baxter glanced at his watch, "Two minutes." He turned the jeep down the trail. "How's the signal?"

"Getting closer," Scott said.

"How long do you think...?" Baxter started to ask.

"We're almost there," Scott said.

Baxter stopped the jeep, turned off the engine. They were surrounded at once by the sound of the wind whirling through and tugging at the tops of the pines around them. In the distance Esbeth heard a sound—an owl, she hoped.

Scott looked up from the gadget. "It went out."

"We'll have to go ahead on foot," Baxter said.

"Can't be far," Scott said. "The signal was bright."

Esbeth was slowest climbing out of the jeep. She heard the motor roaring toward them even as she stepped to the ground.

A minivan careened around the corner of the trail ahead of them and came directly toward the jeep. Its motor was over-revving, as if the driver was stepping on the gas and brake at the same time. Esbeth saw someone on the other side of the jeep dive into a tall stand of briars. The van raced closer, and at the last minute, it spun and slid across the road throwing dirt until it slammed up against the bole of a pine. The driver's door swung open, and the driver tottered out. Baxter and Erickson rushed to the van and grabbed the driver. Esbeth could hear Scott shouting from the briars.

She should have gone to help Scott. But she was drawn to the van. She walked as fast as she could until she was near enough to be sure. Baxter and his deputy had their hands full with the driver who finally turned Esbeth's way in the struggle. It was Mary Elizabeth.

M ary Elizabeth sat sulking, handcuffed and pressed between Ben and Scott in the jeep's back seat, waiting to go to the lodge. It hurt Esbeth as much to see her trussed up that way as it had to find her other two friends dead.

She was a taller woman than Esbeth, but most were. There was still a stubborn bit of gray in her otherwise white hair. She stared straight ahead, the aquiline carving of her face showing very little except the stiff set wrinkles from seventy years of fairly austere living. Back when they had all been in school together, she had an artistic bent, something that never came to much through all the years. Esbeth caught herself glancing back at her, but she acknowledged neither that nor the questions they all had fired at her.

She wore a khaki jumpsuit, the kind she must have been wearing all week as she camped out near the lodge. Just think how cold it must have been up there some nights. They had gone on up the trail a ways and found her campsite, high on a ridge where she could get to the river but in an area where, according to Baxter, you rarely ever encountered bears.

Scott was looking her over too. He said to Esbeth, "I thought you said she had a broken hip?"

"I thought she did," Esbeth said. "Who'd think she'd fake something like that just to get out of a trip she organized herself?" Esbeth thought Mary Elizabeth might rise to the challenge of being talked about as if she weren't there. But that seemed to sail past her too.

Baxter sat at the wheel, but before he started the noisy jeep, he said, "Tell me, Esbeth, how you managed this last piece of fancy footwork."

"The phone bit?" she shrugged. "Most of us would have pointed a finger Mary Elizabeth's way all along if we thought she was the murdering type, which we didn't, or if we thought she was here, which we also didn't. I talked with her in Austin enough, but then I got thinking about those pricey new wireless phones, only out since eighty-three, and how someone can use call forwarding to get calls wherever they might be. But still, I was thinking about that broken hip. We all knew about it, but none of us had checked with Mary Elizabeth's doctor. Who would?"

"There'll be a record of the call forwarding," Baxter said, "and the permit to use the private roads getting back up in here. Then there's the fact of finding her up here. That should pretty much wrap it up."

"It should," Esbeth said, giving Mary Elizabeth another significant glance. Her eyes nearly connected with Esbeth's this time before she looked away. It tore at Esbeth to look at her and talk about her like that. Esbeth kept hoping she would speak up. But the stone faces on Mount Rushmore were chattier than she was being since she got arrested and was read her rights.

Baxter fired up the jeep, and they began the noisy, bouncing ride back to the lodge. There was little more to say, though she still sneaked a look back at Mary Elizabeth now and again, remembering how this was a chatty and warm person, a friend of hers, jostled as much by life as the ride they were on now. But she was someone Esbeth had trusted and been friends with for years.

As they pulled out of the last of the woods, Baxter steered toward the pier, where the boats and planes were bobbing softly, waiting to take Mary Elizabeth away. Esbeth reached out a hand and grabbed Baxter's shoulder, signaling for him to stop a moment.

"Now what is it?" he said.

"Why don't you take her to the lodge for just a bit first?" Esbeth asked.

"But..." Ben started to say something. Baxter waved him quiet. He was staring at Esbeth. "This better be good," he said.

"Are you a betting man?" Scott said from the back seat. It was the first he'd spoken since his brief beefing while picking briars off himself and getting into the jeep.

Baxter gave him a glance that was not full of rosy kindness then looked at Esbeth again. She bent closer and whispered into his ear. His head snapped back then wheeled to Mary Elizabeth. He looked over at the lodge and said to Esbeth, "Why didn't you say that before?"

"You'll make the call?" Esbeth asked.

He sighed. "I guess... Of course I will." To Ben, he said, "We'll make a short detour first. Then you go and get the plane warmed up."

Ben was staring at Esbeth, stunned a bit by seeing his boss take anything like directions from a fossil like her. But he had to know that Baxter was under a lot of pressure to get this mess solved quickly—and right. Though they were somewhat cut off out here, the media had to be kicking up quite a fuss about septuagenarian tourists being killed up in the Allagash Wilderness Waterway. Otherwise, Baxter would have never reversed enough to ask for help from someone like Esbeth. But the look on her face was more sad than smug as the jeep turned and headed toward the lodge.

When they pulled up to the main lodge building, Lamant was on the porch watching them pull up, no doubt fretting about the precious jeep he'd been reluctant to loan them. He stared at them as they climbed out. "You catch the one what done it?" he finally asked.

Mary Elizabeth gave him a glare that would have shriveled a lesser man. But Lamant glared right back at her.

They all climbed out of the jeep, Scott and Ben helping the handcuffed Mary Elizabeth out of the back seat. Once on the ground, the group went inside. Alex came rushing over. Bo Emma sat at one of the tables, eating something. She staggered to her feet, dropped a fork that clattered on the wooden floor. She stared at her ex-mother-in-law, who they had to help into a chair.

Esbeth was looking around at the inside of the lodge, so cozy and home-like with its fireplace and tablecloths, the smells of cooking all around, the knotty pine walls, and the carved chairs. It would seem a nice place to spend a vacation if it had not been for all the craziness and sadness that had happened at the retreat so far.

"Alex," Esbeth said in an aside, "do you think you could get Phyllis to come out here?"

Alex nodded and scurried off toward the kitchen. Esbeth caught Baxter peering at her from under his thick eyebrows, his head lowered as he leaned close to Mary Elizabeth, trying once more to get her to say something.

Phyllis came out of the kitchen, wiping her hands on her apron and sending a puzzled look in our direction. Then her face lit up. "Mary Eliz..." Her smile froze, took in the way the lawmen who were gathered around Mary Elizabeth. She may have even seen the hands cuffed together under the table.

Lamant Willis had just come through the door. He rushed toward them from the other direction, waving his arms at Phyllis, as animated as Esbeth had seen him since arriving up here.

"What gives here?" Baxter grabbed at the slip. "Do you know this woman?" He stood with his attention fixed on Phyllis.

"Yes," Phyllis said. "No."

"Which is it going to be?" Baxter snapped.

"Oh, my heavens!" Garlena shouted. She and Shanna barged in amongst them, must have slipped in during all the confusion. "Mary Elizabeth," Garlena said. "Your hip?" Garlena's eyes swung to Esbeth, more confusion than forgiveness in them. Shanna's eyes stayed wide open.

"Wait a minute," Baxter shouted over the growing confusion.

"I get it," Garlena drowned him out. "She's the one. She's been here all along."

Bo Emma fluttered at the edge of the gathering crowd. She looked uncertain. Scott and Alex stood covering Esbeth's flanks. Almost everyone in the room came closer, adding to the crowd and the chaos. Esbeth didn't know how Mary Elizabeth felt, but Esbeth felt hemmed in. Phyllis and Lamant were in the circle too. They were the ones getting Baxter's unflinching stare.

Baxter finally settled back into his chair and locked stares with Mary Elizabeth. "You've been here before," he said, "haven't you?"

Mary Elizabeth's eyes flicked up to Lamant then Phyllis. Lamant glared. Phyllis was biting her lip. Then Mary Elizabeth's head turned slowly until she was staring at Esbeth.

"Unless you say something," Esbeth said, "you stand a good chance of getting stuck with the murders." She blinked, and Esbeth saw her jaw tighten.

She swallowed then opened her mouth, but her first effort to speak didn't make it—rusty pipes or something.

"Do you want water, coffee?" Esbeth said.

She shook her head, pressed her lips more tightly together than before. Phyllis, seeing that she wasn't needed, hurried from the room back toward the kitchen.

Esbeth stared hard at Mary Elizabeth, whose head swung away. She stared off at nothing, a single tear running down across one cheek.

Esbeth looked at Baxter and shook her head.

He gave her an eyebrow shrug, turned to Ben, and said, "You better fire up the plane. I've got to put through a call."

Ben looked far gladder than Esbeth felt as he hurried off, eager to be doing something. Esbeth took a last look at Mary Elizabeth, hoped she could see the pleading in her eyes. But she ignored Esbeth with a will larger than all their years of knowing each other.

As it got darker that evening, it gradually became the chilliest it had been since they'd arrived. The plane and Mary Elizabeth had long departed. Scott, Alex, and Esbeth huddled near the big fireplace in the dining room. Garlena, Shanna, and Bo Emma had gathered at the nearest table, all having apologized to Esbeth earlier. Their friendships renewed, they had their heads close together now, talking, no doubt about the same things Alex, Scott, and Esbeth discussed by the fire. Lamant sat off in his corner at his usual table, smoke from his pipe surrounding him in an anti-social cloud.

"Try as hard as I might," Alex said, "I can't begin to *imagine* what drives a person to not only want to kill another person but to actually do it."

"You think Esbeth has a morbid hobby?" Scott asked. He had been sitting quietly, doing what he did best—listening and sharing his attention.

Alex gave a delicate shudder. Flickers from the fire animated the smooth lines of her young face, highlighting her short-cropped hair. She was far from naive, but Esbeth was still full enough with grief to appreciate her response more than resent it.

"Before we came up here," Scott said after another silent stretch, "I was called to a crime scene in Austin. A two-and-a-half-year-old girl died of a ruptured liver. The ME got called in. Looks like the case'll be handled by Homicide." He sighed, looking off into the fire.

Alex and Esbeth looked at each other then at him.

"I've been to more scenes like that than I'd like to remember. Young or old, it's never anything I fully understand. It's like we all have a touch or two of gunpowder in us, but some of us wrap it tighter and tighter, suppress it long enough until there's a shorter and shorter fuse." He stood up abruptly. "Oh, what the... I guess I can't explain it." He looked at Alex then Esbeth. World-weariness showed for one of the few times in his laconic life that he showed anything close to what went on inside that stone head of his.

"I think it's time for me to head for the hay." He struggled for something close to a grin.

"It's time," Esbeth said.

He slumped off through the room. Only a head or two rose to note his parting. There were still a couple of hours to go before lights out. After he'd been gone a few minutes, Esbeth pushed herself to her feet.

"Guess I'd better turn in too," she told Alex. "You going to stay a while?" Alex nodded. Esbeth gave the others at their table a good-night wave. As she turned to leave, Alex reached out a hand and gave her arm a brief squeeze. "Be careful," she said. Esbeth nodded.

Esbeth had made only a few steps toward the door when a shout from Bo Emma stopped her. Esbeth turned, and all three of them were waving her to their table. Esbeth glanced around, but though the knotty pine walls were spotted with all manner of dead fish, fowl, and beast, she saw no clock.

Well, she didn't have so many friends that she could ignore the few she had. She went over to the table.

"Guys," Esbeth said before any of them could wedge in more than another hello, "I feel like I've been drawn through a knothole backward. I just want to get to my cabin."

Garlena and Shanna's heads both moved back an inch, but Bo Emma's was too irrepressible a spirit to take any affront. "Esbeth, it's just like you to be a shy and retiring hero. I was just telling the others again how you saved my bacon out there. And I'm the first to admit my bacon was shakin'." She laughed at herself, and Shanna and Garlena both relaxed.

"Sit down and trade lies, Esbeth. Come on," Garlena said. "The coffee's so weak we had to help it out of the pot. I don't know what's up with Phyllis back there. But at least it won't keep you up."

"Oh, Garlena," Shanna said, as laughing and bubbly as Esbeth ever remembered seeing her, "you're enough to make a cat laugh." There was something about just missing the swinging sickle of the Grim Reaper and knowing that you were safe again that can make anyone giddy.

"Maybe tomorrow," Esbeth said. "Please. Let me beg off this once." There was something in the tone of her voice that encouraged them not to press her to stay.

"Well, thanks again for saving me," Bo Emma said.

"And us as well," Shanna tossed in. Esbeth wished she could have gathered some joy from it all.

As she walked away from the table, she heard Garlena saying, "Myself, I was born tired and suffer relapses." Esbeth could still hear Bo Emma giggling as Esbeth slipped out the door into the crisp dark night.

It was cold outside. She clutched her sweater close and hurried along the crunching walk until she was inside the cabin. There was only the dim red glow from the Franklin stove. She didn't light either of the room's two lanterns, just banged around for a couple of minutes in the semi-dark and settled in.

A very long twenty minutes ticked by.

The logs of the cabin creaked. Pine branches rustled in the wind outside, scraped against the wood. Then there was a soft crunch of gravel.

She'd left the door unlocked for Alex. The oiled latch lifted slowly, barely made the soft sound of metal sliding. The door swung open to a crack then opened all the way. A crouching figure slipped into the room, moved silently and quickly across the shadows and faint red glow toward the bundled figure on the chair pulled close to the stove.

Even though Esbeth's eyes had adjusted to the dim light, it was hard to make out the movement. An arm seemed to lift high, holding something that reflected metallically in the pale light. Then the arm crashed down, and the figure slumped to the floor. The arm rose again for another blow. There was a blinding flash of white then another.

In the lightning flash of the camera's bulb, Esbeth caught a strobe-light glimpse of the turned face, the recognized terror of being caught in the act. She heard the metal bar drop to the cabin floor. There was a scurry of footsteps and a scuffle. Esbeth had her shaky hands full lighting the match she held, getting the kerosene lamp lit.

As she turned up the wick, the room was bathed in a haunting yellow light. Dark figures wrestled just inside the doorway. Struggling grunts were all Esbeth heard from the bottom of the pile. Sheriff Baxter was on top, one of the cuffs already on. He and Scott wrestled to get the other arm around. As they clasped it in place and stood back, Esbeth saw the animal fear and hate on Lamant's face. He struggled for just a moment more then collapsed in a panting glare, breathing hard but saying nothing.

Scott glanced over to make sure the camera he'd eased to the floor hadn't been damaged as he had joined in the fracas. Then he gave Baxter a hand in getting the now surly but defeated Lamant to his feet. Baxter read Lamant his rights in a steady monotone. Lamant's jaw muscles twitched, and he glared, but he was too spent to do more than that.

"You might as well know," Baxter said to the lodge manager, "that Mary Elizabeth, your sister, talked after all."

Lamant gave a brief struggle but settled when Baxter gave him a firm yank. "She told us she didn't do it, that she'd only come up and hovered around the camp trying to prevent the killings, told us that in her visits up here through all these years that you were getting bitter, meaner, that all she wanted to do was protect you."

Scott glanced at Esbeth, who shrugged. The man was probably beyond communication.

Baxter turned on the walkie-talkie at his belt, turned up the squelch, and keyed the mike. "Bring the plane around, Ben," he said into it.

To Scott, he said, "You mind giving me a hand getting him to the pier? I'm going to need that film too."

While Scott went over and fiddled with his camera, taking out the film, Baxter gripped Lamant firmly and shook his head at me. "You are a wonder, Esbeth, and certainly work in mysterious ways. It took some real favor trading, but you were on the money. He *was* in the Witness Protection Program. But how did you know?"

Esbeth stood exhausted and emotionally spent but resisted tottering over to one of the chairs Lamant hadn't smashed. The iron bar he'd used still lay on the floor. Baxter would have to take it in, would no doubt find some of Noreen's blood on it. Esbeth didn't want to look at it, or at Lamant, for that matter. But she was fascinated. It had been well over fifty years since she'd seen him—had, like everyone else, supposed he was dead.

"It's the only way it made sense," Esbeth said.

Scott handed Baxter the film from his camera in a tin container and gripped Lamant's other arm. Esbeth could hear a plane now approaching from a distance.

"Mary Elizabeth knew her way around up here too well," Esbeth said, "could even get by in the woods, old as she is. Phyllis knew her. Mary Elizabeth must have visited often. Lamant seemed to despise it up here. But he couldn't leave. Title 18 of the US Code for Crimes and Criminal Procedure passed in 1948. By the 1950s, some people were already being moved around the country under the provisions of Chapter 224—what we now know as the Witness Protection Program. He must have been one of the early people transported. Larry became Lamant Willis. I know when you're in it, you're not supposed to maintain any contact with people from your former life. But blood's sometimes thicker than all that. Imagine too how lonely it must have seemed up here, especially to someone like Larry, who had once been drawn to the lights and action of cities He must have gotten in touch with Mary Elizabeth after staying up here got too much for him."

"That clicks with what she's told us so far," Baxter nodded. He started to tug Lamant toward the door. "Don't touch that spud." He indicated the metal bar on the floor. "I'll be back for that. We have hard evidence now we'd have never had if we'd handled this my way."

"You're welcome," Esbeth said softly to herself as he and Scott disappeared out the door.

She heard a short shriek a few moments later then, "Dad! Dad! Where are they taking you?" She felt bad for Phyllis. She felt as lousy for herself.

Alex came in the door just as Esbeth was plopping into a chair. "Whew!" Alex said. "It went well?" She looked around the room, took in the shattered chair and smashed dummy they'd put together earlier.

"It went," Esbeth sighed.

Alex didn't say anything, just came and put a hand on Esbeth's shoulder.

Esbeth was past crying, too tired or still in a daze. But she couldn't quite shut herself up.

"Abby must have recognized him, or thought she did," Esbeth said, "maybe followed him to the river where he took supplies across the dam to where Mary Elizabeth was camped. He caught her somehow, killed her like he killed Noreen, lashing out at other people, bitter at the way he'd lived, maybe, or perhaps at the way he thought Mary Elizabeth had been treated by all of us. Living away from where he wanted to be must have stewed in him to such a level of resentment for so many years I wonder if he even knew what he hated. Maybe in some twisted way, we all represented what he'd been cut off from. Mary Elizabeth must have known or sensed how near the edge he was. Oh, I don't know, can't say, and am not even sure if I care."

"You don't need to say anything just now."

A wisp of wind flared up Franklin's fire and lit the room in red for a moment.

"All we'll ever know from our end," Esbeth said, "is that Mary Elizabeth's brother quit school early, like a lot of fellows did back then. Some took up farming. Others went out to work as hands on ranches. Some went to the oil fields. What we heard about Larry, or Lamant, is that he went to Houston or San Antonio. Others said Dallas. None of that matters much. He was always a hustler, even then. Word got back to Austin that he'd been mixed up in a little trouble, then we never heard another thing about him. This was ten or fifteen years after he left Austin. World War II had been over for just a few years. I think Larry had served, came back with some black market connections or something. Everything we heard was garbled, secondhand."

Esbeth paused. Alex might have sensed that Esbeth was letting some of this go, easing some pain of inner knowledge with which she was struggling. Esbeth knew now why she had wanted Scott and her close, that she had sensed by then how this might go, that it was not going to be pretty or pleasant.

"And think of poor Mary Elizabeth. For years, this was her secret, coming up here, stealing visits. But"—and this was one of the hardest things with which Esbeth had to deal—"Mary Elizabeth did set the whole trip up, lured us all up here. Then she had come up herself, in a somewhat elaborate subterfuge. I don't know if it was to watch us be killed, or if she really did want to prevent it like she said." Esbeth let out an exhausted sigh.

If you've ever told a spellbinder around a campfire and watched the fixed faces staring at you, then you know the quick wide-eyed glance Esbeth got from Alex. But behind that was a flicker Esbeth had often seen in Scott's face, and that was of genuine care, and if anything was going to get her through all this, that was it.

Esbeth looked up into the face of her friend and said, "I do think now that I'm going to have a whole new meaning to remembering Maine."

About the Author

Russ Hall is author of fifteen published fiction books, most in hardback and subsequently published in mass market paperback by Harlequin's Worldwide Mystery imprint and Leisure Books. He has also co-authored numerous non-fiction books, most recently *Do You Matter: How Great Design Will Make People Love Your Company* (Financial Times Press, 2009) with Richard Brunner, former head of design at Apple, *Now You're Thinking* (Financial Times Press, 2011), and *Identity* (Financial Times Press, 2012) with Stedman Graham, Oprah's companion.

His graduate degree is in creative writing. He has been a nonfiction editor for major publishing companies, ranging from HarperCollins (then Harper & Row), Simon & Schuster, to Pearson. He has lived in Columbus, OH, New Haven, CT, Boca Raton, FL, Chapel Hill, NC, and New York City. Moving to the Austin area from New York City in 1983.

He is a long-time member of the Mystery Writers of America, Western Writers of America, and Sisters in Crime. He is a frequent judge for writing organizations.

In 2011, he was awarded the Sage Award, by The Barbara Burnett Smith Mentoring Authors Foundation—a Texas award for the mentoring author who demonstrates an outstanding spirit of service in mentoring, sharing and leading others in the mystery writing community. In 1996, he won the Nancy Pickard Mystery Fiction Award for short fiction.

Read more at www.russhall.com.

About the Publisher

Dear Reader,

We hope you enjoyed this book. Please consider leaving a review on your favorite book site.

Visit https://RedAdeptPublishing.com to see our entire catalogue.

Check out our app for short stories, articles, and interviews. You'll also be notified of future releases and special sales.